L

WARNING:
O NOT GIVE THIS BOOK TO YOUR OWN GRANDMA. SHE MIGHT GET IDEAS.

ORCHARD BOOKS

First published in Great Britain in 2018 by The Watts Publishing Group

1 3 5 7 9 10 8 6 4 2

Text copyright © Kita Mitchell 2019
Illustrations © Nathan Reed 2019

The moral rights of the author and illustrator have been asserted.

A CIP catalogue record for this book
is available from the British Library.

ISBN 978 1 40835 550 3

Printed and bound in Great Britain by
CPI Group (UK) Ltd, Croydon, CR0 4YY

The paper and board used in this book are
made from wood from responsible sources.

Orchard Books
An imprint of Hachette Children's Group
Part of The Watts Publishing Group Limited
Carmelite House
50 Victoria Embankment
London EC4Y 0DZ

An Hachette UK Company
www.hachette.co.uk
www.hachettechildrens.co.uk

GRANDMA DANGEROUS AND THE EGG OF GLORY

By Kita Mitchell

Illustrated by Nathan Reed

ORCHARD

For Isobel, Eva, Hattie & Daisy

'Sorry?' I said. 'Did I hear that right?'

'I thought you'd be pleased,' Mum said. 'You said you were bored yesterday.' She unfolded the camp bed alongside mine. 'He'll only be here a week.'

'But it's Thomas,' I said. **'Thomas.'** I looked at her in horror. **'You know we don't get on.'**

'You didn't get along at Christmas.' Mum busied herself with a pillow. 'That was *months* ago.'

'He'll be just as annoying,' I said. 'Why can't he stay with one of his other cousins?'

Mum looked sheepish. 'They're all busy.'

'I bet they're not,' I said. 'They'll have just said that so they didn't have to listen to him going on and on, ruining their holidays.'

'Don't be mean.' Mum straightened the sheet. 'It must be hard for him. His parents are always away.

Boarding school can't be much fun.'

'I don't know about that,' I said. 'Aunt Sarah says it's the **best boarding school in the world**. Apparently it's got a one-hundred-metre swimming pool, and Leonardo DiCaprio runs the drama department.'

'She was exaggerating,' Mum said. 'The pool's only fifty metres. I looked on the website.'

Fifty metres is still **massive!** My school doesn't even have a paddling pool! (I suppose there's quite a big tank in the science room, but that has frogspawn in it.)

Mum went on, 'He's doing very well. Sarah says he's top of the class in almost every subject.'

'There's a surprise,' I muttered.

Thomas is the same age as me, but that's the only thing we have in common. He's ever so annoying. He spent the whole of Christmas putting things on plates and offering them round. If there was a championship in sucking up, he would definitely win it.

Aunt Sarah's always going on about how clever he is.

Once I overheard her say she wouldn't be surprised if he became Prime Minister! Then she asked Mum if she thought I'd pass my SATs!!! **What a cheek!**

I'd been going to spend this week treasure hunting with Piper. She found a metal detector in her grandad's shed, and we had stacks of plans.

Now Thomas was coming to stay, Mum would organise all sorts of rubbish stuff.

Things like board games, and blow football, and **CRAFT.**

I wasn't going to win the *'What I Did in My Holidays'* essay competition by writing about something I made from an egg box, was I?

Mrs Jones had told us about the competition on the last day of school.

She said the prize was two tickets to the cinema and *'all you can eat'* at Great Potton Pizza Palace, afterwards.

If I'd won, I might have invited Thea Harris.

There was **no chance** of that **now**.

Mum was still talking. 'If he says anything that annoys you,' she said, 'count to ten or ... I don't know. Offer him a biscuit. I've got some in, specially.' She looked at me. 'Just try and be nice.'

Mum doesn't normally approve of biscuits (trans fats) so it was good to hear she'd bought some – **but, be nice?** Sharing my room was hard enough! I mean, I could try, but I wasn't sure I'd be able to keep it up for a whole week.

'Oh.' Mum looked a bit shifty.

'What?' I asked.

'Myrtle,' she said. 'I'm afraid you'll have to move her downstairs. He's allergic to hamsters. Anything with fur, in fact.'

Eh? I blinked in disbelief. Was she kidding? Myrtle

had more right to be in my room than Thomas! Perhaps HE could go downstairs?

'I'll move her later,' I said. 'I've got to go. I'm meeting Piper.'

'Well, make sure you're back by three. And don't forget your phone.' Mum looked anxious. 'Text me when you get there, won't you?'

'Mum. The park is two minutes from our house.'

'Even so. You know I worry.'

'Mum. I'm **eleven**.'

Mum worries about everything. She says if I was ever kidnapped, or fell down a mineshaft, or got Ebola from a Mr Whippy, she'd never forgive herself.

She's better than she used to be. She's stopped trying to hold my hand when we cross the road. And I'm even allowed out by myself – as long as she knows exactly where I'm going, the names, addresses and heights of everyone I'm with, and the precise millisecond I'll be home.

I felt cross about Thomas all the way to the park.
Piper wouldn't be pleased. I'd told her about him
after Christmas – and I hadn't even exaggerated –
and she said he sounded awful.

I've known Piper for ages. She's in my year at
school. She's quite annoying too, but to be fair, she's
never been as annoying as Thomas.

There she was. Over by the bandstand, with a
supermarket trolley. She wasn't hard to spot. She
doesn't wear her hair in pigtails any more, and it's
got ever so big, as well as being ever so ginger.

If she wanted to be an undercover policeman, or
a spy, she'd have to dye it, or wear an enormous hat.

She saw me and waved. **'Hurry up!'** she shouted.
'I've been here ages.'

I sped up. 'Do Tesco know you've got that?'

'It's mine. I paid a pound for it.' She pushed the trolley towards me. 'I've got everything we need, I think.'

I peered into it. As well as the metal detector, there were several spades, a sieve and a plastic box with **'treasure'** written on the lid in purple pen.

'We have to take this seriously,' Piper said. 'I'm saving up.'

'What for?' I asked.

'A caravan.'

'Eh?' I looked at her. 'Why do you want a caravan?'

'It's really crowded in my house. I'm fed up with sharing. I need my own space.'

I thought bitterly about the camp bed. 'I know what you mean,' I said.

Piper looked cross. 'How can you?' she said. 'It's only you and Myrtle.'

'Not for much longer,' I said. 'There's something I need to tell you.'

'OMG!' Piper gave a shriek and grabbed me. 'Is

your mum having a baby?'

I swear **EVERY** person in the park turned around. Mrs Briggs, who lives two doors down and was walking her dog ahead of us, definitely heard.

'Piper,' I hissed.

Piper looked disappointed. 'She isn't?'

'NO.'

'Well, what's wrong, then?' she said. 'Because if you've just come here to look miserable, I'm quite happy to go treasure hunting by myself. I won't have to split the proceeds.'

'It's Thomas.'

'Thomas?'

'Yes,' I said. 'Thomas. My cousin. He's coming to stay.'

'Thomas?' Piper looked at me. 'Thomas from Christmas? The one who had voluntary seconds of sprouts? The one who did the washing up even though you've got a dishwasher, just to **suck up**? The one you moaned on about for ages? The posh one? That Thomas?'

I nodded mournfully.

'How long's he here for?'

'The whole week.'

Piper raised her eyebrows. 'I'm not going thirds on any treasure,' she said. 'You'll have to share your half.'

'He might not want to come,' I said. 'He'll have been treasure hunting before. I expect his finds are on display at the British Museum.' I kicked at a tuft of grass. 'Great Potton Park won't meet his expectations.'

'You may as well bring him,' Piper said. 'As long as he knows I'm **not** sharing. He can help with the digging.'

'I'm sure he'll tell you where to dig,' I said. 'And that you're doing your digging wrong, but I bet he won't dig.'

Piper shrugged. 'He can push the trolley then.' She reached for the metal detector. 'We'd better get on if you've got to get back.'

I looked at all the dials. 'How does it work?'

She flicked a switch. 'There's two settings,' she said. 'One for "All Metals", and this one,' she turned a knob, 'for "Gold and Silver".'

I thought we should use that setting, but Piper didn't agree.

'There's an Iron Age and a Bronze Age,' she said. 'We don't want to miss anything.' She looked around. 'Right. Where would someone bury their hoard, and then forget about it?'

I pointed at a large oak. 'By that tree, definitely.'

We found a place between the roots that looked likely, and Piper started to sweep the detector over the ground.

It beeped almost immediately!

Woohoo!

I grabbed a trowel and started digging. Primroses flew everywhere. The ground wasn't very soft, though, and there was loads of tree in the way.

'You're not getting very far,' Piper said, eventually. 'Shall I have a go?'

I was just about to say that she jolly well could do some of the hard work, when the trowel hit something.

Piper almost knocked me over.

'What is it?' She peered into the hole.

'A stone,' I said. 'Could you move out of the way?'

'Sorry.'

I dug a bit more. I hoped the treasure wasn't much deeper. I was getting a blister. I was going to suggest that Piper take over when I saw a glint in the soil.

YAY! I threw down the trowel and reached into the hole.

Piper clapped her hands in excitement.

'Hurry!' she said.

I pulled out the object and looked at it.

Whatever it was, was tiny, and encrusted with dirt.

I scraped some off.

Piper squealed. She covered her mouth with her hands. **'OMG, Ollie,'** she said. **'It's a medieval brooch!'**

I looked at her. 'It's a ring-pull.'

'Oh.' She poked at it. 'So it is. Never mind. Let's try somewhere else. How about over by that flowerbed?'

We'd managed to dig up eight more ring-pulls, a sparkly hair clip and a key before the park-keeper came over.

He wasn't very friendly. Piper explained about the caravan, but it didn't make any difference.

Apparently, 'holes' are not allowed in Great Potton Park, under any circumstances.

Piper argued with him for a bit, but he said if she didn't take her spade and **buzz off**, he'd report her for stealing a trolley.

'I paid a pound for it, actually,' Piper shouted after him. She scowled. 'Come on. Let's go. There's loads of better places.'

I checked the time on my phone. 'I can't,' I said. 'It's nearly three.'

'Oh. OK.' Piper started collecting her stuff together. 'I'll come with you.'

'Really?' I said. 'Why?'

'To see if Thomas is as bad as you say.'

'He is,' I said.

Piper giggled. 'I guess he's from your mum's side?'

'Yep,' I said.

Of course he was.

Mum's side of the family are all **TOTALLY SQUARE.**

Mum's a health and safety officer for Great Potton Council. She's very good at her job. Great Potton is now the safest place in the country.

Grandma Boring – sorry, Grandma Beatrix, who is Mum's mum, gave me a maths revision book for my last birthday. That took my 'pretending to be pleased' skills to a whole new level. I must have been convincing, though, as I got the next in the series for Christmas.

Thomas is the worst. **He's actually squarer than square.** He wears shirts and waistcoats, and sometimes, if he feels like it, a little bow tie.

No one related to Dad would ever wear a bow tie.

Dad's an explorer. He mainly wears shorts, and flies around in a plane he built himself. He's just got back from America, where he was demonstrating an engine he invented. Mum likes it when he's home, as it means we know where he is. (Sometimes we don't and that can be worrying.)

Dad's mum, Grandma Florence, is an explorer too.

Grandma Florence is brilliant. She's tall and loud, with a really big nose. Sometimes she brushes her hair, but not very often.

She's SO much fun.

I haven't seen her for ages. Last time she came over, she said she was off to Russia. But she could just as likely be in Clacton. To be honest, **she could be anywhere.**

I hope she's not in any trouble.

I'm not sure if I inherited any explorer genes or not. I think I have. I'm OK with the slide at Great Potton Pool, and I'm pretty good with wildlife. I mean, Myrtle's six, and most hamsters only make it to two, so I must be doing something right. (Her coat does change colour occasionally, which is freaky, but Mum says that's completely normal for elderly rodents.)

I'm not great in the heat, though – **AND I DON'T LIKE SPIDERS**, even ones that aren't poisonous.

Grandma says that explorer genes need to be developed, and Mum should let me do more fun stuff.

Mum doesn't agree. She wants me to be an **accountant.**

Grandma Florence makes her nervous. Behind her back, Mum calls her Grandma Dangerous.

Honestly! Grandma's not that dangerous. She

crashed her hot-air balloon once! And it was my idea to put the firework in the trifle on Bonfire Night. Grandma only lit it. We even stood well back, like it said on the box.

How were we supposed to know a pudding could go so far?

We cleaned up and everything, but Grandma wasn't invited for a while after that.

'He's here,' I said, as we turned into my street.

'How do you know?' Piper asked.

I pointed at the limo driving off.

'Blimey,' Piper said. 'That's nice.'

'It's his parents' car,' I said. 'They're away, but they have a **chauffeur.**'

'Oh my.' Piper looked impressed. 'I've never met anyone with a chauffeur. I'm surprised he's coming to stay with you, Ollie. Doesn't he have better relatives he could stay with?'

'They were all busy,' I said. 'Well, they **said** they were, anyway.'

I hoped Thomas was wearing his bow tie. It would be a shame if Piper didn't get to see it.

We parked the trolley on the drive.

'Put the brake on,' Piper said. 'We don't want it

rolling off. It's still got my pound in.'

There was so much luggage in the hallway we could barely get in through the door. He'd brought quite a lot, considering he was only staying a week.

'**Who's Gucci?**' Piper asked, staring at the cases. 'I thought his name was Thomas?'

'I think Gucci made them,' I said.

'Why would you want a name on something if it wasn't your name?' Piper said. 'And it matches.' She looked quite amazed. 'I've never met anyone with matching luggage.'

Thomas was sitting at the kitchen table, sipping his tea out of a teacup. The teacup had a saucer, and after every sip he put the cup back on to it.

I didn't even know we had saucers. Or a teapot. **Blimey**. Anyone would think the **queen** was coming.

Dad was there too. Mum must have had a word, because he looked quite smart for a change.

'Hi, you two,' he said.

Mum told me off for being **thirty seconds** late.

'Sorry,' I said. 'There were some bags in the way. Hi, Thomas.'

'Ollie. **Wonderful** to see you.' Thomas put down his tea and held out his hand. 'It's been too long.'

It hadn't been long enough, in my opinion, but I pretended I was pleased to see him anyway.

He was still **small** and **smug-looking**. He'd left off his bow tie, which was a shame, but he was wearing a knitted tank top over a pink shirt, which more than made up for it. His hair had grown quite long and curled up around his collar. I was surprised he was allowed it like that at his school. They're very strict about hair at Great Potton Primary. Especially since the World Book Day incident.

I mean, it wasn't really anyone's fault. I'd gone as Tintin, and Grandma had lent me some superglue to spike my fringe up.

It looked really good, so loads of people asked to use it. (It was quite a big tube, so I didn't mind.)

Grandma had said it would wash out.

It didn't.

Thea Harris hasn't spoken to me since.

Dad introduced Piper to Thomas. 'Have you met before?' he asked.

'No,' Piper said. 'But I've heard **loads** about him.'

Thomas beamed at her. 'All good, I hope?'

'Oh yes.' Piper nodded. 'Very.'

Mum gave me a suspicious look.

I pretended not to see it. 'Another cake?' I offered Thomas the plate.

'Why, thank you.' He took one. 'These are **delicious**, Aunt Sukey.'

'I'm glad you like them.' Mum pushed her chair back. 'Right. Dad and I'll make a start on the bags. Help yourself to more tea. It's hot, though, so use the oven gloves.'

'I'll pour.' Piper admired the teapot. 'We don't have one of these. At home we just put teabags straight into cups.'

'We **normally** do that.' I looked pointedly at Thomas.

'It's polite to make an effort for visitors, Ollie.' Piper slopped tea on the table. 'Even my mum does. Once, she hoovered.' She looked at Thomas. 'I expect you have servants, being so rich?'

Thomas looked uncomfortable. 'Mum might have a cleaner,' he said. 'I don't know. I don't see her much.'

'I don't see mine much either,' said Piper. 'She's **always** busy. You'd think four children would be enough, wouldn't you, but then she had another one, which turned out to be twins. I don't mind really. They're quite cute.'

I started to feel cross. I thought Piper had come to see how annoying Thomas was, not chat away like she'd known him for years!

'How's school, Thomas?' I asked. Ha. Now she'd see. Thomas could go on for hours about school.

'School?' Thomas blinked. 'Excellent. I'm very lucky to be there. Piper? Could I trouble you for another cup of tea?'

Piper walked around with the teapot. 'Ollie says you get ten different sorts of pudding,' she said. 'Do you really?'

'Oh, yes.' Thomas sat up straighter. 'Fifteen at weekends. It's terribly hard to choose.'

'Wow,' Piper said. 'I might apply.'

'Really?' Thomas took a dainty nibble of his cake. 'Well, it's a very good school. My parents like its motto. "**Vincere est Totum**".'

'Eh?' Piper said.

'It's Latin,' explained Thomas. 'It means "**Winning is Everything**". Then underneath, in brackets, it says "Only Losers Lose".'

Piper looked confused. 'But not everyone can win,

all the time,' she said. 'That would be impossible.'

'Not according to my school,' said Thomas. He put down his tea. 'We mustn't let Aunt and Uncle do all the work,' he said. 'Shall we go and help?'

I rolled my eyes. Such a suck-up.

Once we'd dragged the rest of Thomas's stuff upstairs, and Mum was showing him where to put things, Piper and I went back to the kitchen.

Dad was in there, finishing off the cakes. 'I need to fill up,' he explained. 'I'm off to Antarctica in a minute. A rare penguin's been spotted. It needs to be logged.'

I bet the penguin didn't need to be logged. Dad had just had enough of Thomas.

When I said that to Piper, she told me off for being mean. 'Thomas isn't that bad,' she said. 'You do exaggerate.'

'Try sharing a room with him,' I said. 'Didn't you see? There's **waistcoats** everywhere.'

I'd have gone into more detail about Thomas's annoying habits but Mum came down to check Dad had packed his woolly hat and factor one million sun cream.

I didn't bother asking if I could go with him. There wasn't any point. I'd **never** be allowed.

'Bye, Ollie.' Dad was being annoyingly cheerful. 'See you soon.'

'Bye,' I muttered.

This was turning into a really rubbish week.

Once Mum had stopped fussing about whether Dad had remembered his parachute or not, (he had), she started to clear the tea things away. Piper offered to help, so I did too, even though I'd been planning to leave it for Thomas.

'Thanks.' Mum pulled open the dishwasher. 'Oh,' she said. 'Did Dad say? Grandma called. She's coming for tea.'

I closed my eyes. Could things get any worse? I should have known Grandma Boring would be over. She loves Thomas. 'Such wonderful manners,' she coos.

I couldn't put up with both of them. I'd have to

pretend I was getting a cold, and go to bed early.

I gave a little cough, followed by a sniff.

Mum went on. 'She's promised to be on her best behaviour.'

'Isn't she always?' I said. I coughed again.

'She's bringing a friend. She didn't say who.' Mum looked around. 'I might just move anything breakable.' She picked up a vase. 'Is something wrong, Ollie? I thought you'd be excited. You haven't seen Grandma Florence for ages.'

I almost dropped a cup. **Grandma Florence? YAY!**

That pretty much made up for Dad going away, and Thomas.

I did a little dance.

It was **SO** great to see Grandma again. She bustled in in her yeti coat (the one with a label that says *Made in Basingstoke*) and gave me a hug. She said she'd really missed me.

She'd brought **Rose**. He trotted behind her, looking as scruffy as ever.

Rose is Grandma's dog. He's actually a boy, but once, we had to disguise him as a girl, and he seemed to like the name.

Piper grabbed him and held him up. **'OMG,'** she said. 'You gave him a haircut, Ollie's gran. Look at his **adorable** fringe. Have you ever seen anything so cute?' She shoved him under Thomas's nose.

Thomas sneezed. 'Sorry,' he said. 'I'm allergic. Is it a chihuahua? It's tiny.'

'He's an Egyptian Choodle.' Piper looked proud. 'A Dog of Destiny. A teller of fortune and bringer of luck. He's very rare. It says so on Wikipedia.'

'Oh, what a delightful fable.' Thomas clasped his hands.

'A fable?' Grandma rushed over to cover Rose's ears. 'It's not a fable, Thomas. You mustn't offend him. Suppose you need him to cast his **lucky aura** over you?'

'His lucky aura?' Thomas looked surprised. 'Do dogs have those?' He sneezed again. 'I expect I'd be allergic to that as well.'

Grandma hung up her coat and introduced her friend.

'This is Edna,' she said. 'We're working together.'

'Lovely to meet you,' Mum said. 'Take a seat. I've made scones.'

'Fabby,' Edna said. She plonked herself down at the table. 'I love a scone.'

Edna was short, and stocky, and had a red face and

a bristly chin. She was wearing an oversized duffel coat with the hood up, though the toggles were undone. Underneath, written on her T-shirt, were the words 'I am Banksy'.

'Are you really?' Piper sat next to her.

'Might be,' Edna said.

'If you were,' I said, 'you **wouldn't** be wearing that.'

'Might,' Edna said. 'Throw them off the scent, wouldn't it?'

'Who?'

'Anyone that might be looking for someone. Not that anyone is.'

'Definitely not.' Grandma nodded in agreement.

'Can I take your coat?' Mum asked Edna.

'No,' she said. 'I'll keep it on. Are those the scones?' She helped herself to one and took a large bite. 'Bit dry,' she mumbled, spraying crumbs everywhere.

Thomas was staring at her with his mouth open. Then he remembered himself and shut it. He nervously picked up his napkin and tucked it into his tank top.

He looked around the table. 'Can I help anyone to anything?' he said. 'Florence? Edna?'

'How kind.' Grandma beamed at him. 'But I can reach everything perfectly well from here.' She leant across for the sugar bowl. Her scarf trailed through the butter. 'Lovely manners,' she whispered to Mum. 'Charming.'

'Yes.' Mum nodded. 'Isn't he. Let me find you a spoon for that sugar.'

'No need.' Grandma tipped the contents of the bowl into her cup. She used her knife to stir it.

Thomas looked **aghast**.

Grandma took a noisy gulp and turned to me.

'How are things here then, Ollie? All OK?'

'Pretty much, thanks, Grandma,' I said. I could hardly moan about guests when they were sitting next to me, could I?

'How lovely to have your cousin staying.' Grandma took another gulp of tea and gargled with it. 'Are you enjoying yourself, Thomas?'

'It's very kind of Sukey to have me,' Thomas said weakly.

'Shove the scones this way, will you?' sprayed Edna.

Thomas closed his eyes. He looked quite faint.

This was great!

'Oh.' Grandma clapped her hands. 'I almost forgot! I've an announcement to make.'

'OMG.' Piper shot up from under the table, where she'd been playing with Rose. 'Are you getting married?'

'Married?' Grandma looked horrified. 'Gracious, Piper. I'd **never** do that. I'm an independent lady. The shackles of matrimony are not on my bucket list.'

'Oh.' Piper looked disappointed. 'That's a shame. I wanted to be a bridesmaid.'

'Sorry, dear.' Grandma patted her on the shoulder. 'But never mind. My announcement is far more exciting than wearing a puffy dress.' She looked around the table.

We all waited.

Grandma took a dramatic breath.

'I'm retiring,' she said.

5

My mouth dropped open. Eh? What? No!

Grandma **couldn't** retire! I hadn't developed my explorer genes yet!

'Are you really?' Piper sat up. 'Can I buy your balloon?'

'Why?' I asked. 'You **love** exploring.'

'It's all been done.' Grandma looked mournful. 'There's no challenge in it any more. I mean, now, if I want to see somewhere, I can just ask Siri.'

OMG. She meant it!

'Even your dad's diversified, Ollie,' Grandma went on. 'He's practically an eco-warrior now, inventing things to save the planet. When was the last time he went anywhere new?'

She had a point – but even so! She could have discussed it with **me** first!

37

'I feel I need to do something – how shall I put it?' Grandma looked thoughtful. **'Worthwhile.'**

Mum looked delighted. 'Well, that's fantastic to hear!' she said. 'You won't regret it, Florence. There's so much round here for oldies to do – and I can teach you to knit if you like?'

'How kind, Sukey,' Grandma said. 'But no need to worry. My retirement is going to be very busy indeed. I have **SO** many plans.'

'What are they?' Piper asked. 'Don't forget I'm top of the list for the balloon.'

Grandma leant forward. She clasped her hands. 'I'm going to give something back,' she said.

'Give something back?' I said. 'What did you steal this time?'

Grandma looked annoyed. 'If you're referring to the recent doughnut incident, Ollie – that was the fault of the supermarket. They should have made it quite clear their baked goods were **not** free samples.'

'An easy mistake to make.' Thomas patted her arm.

'Supermarket signage is terribly misleading.'

'Thank you, Thomas.' Grandma gave him a little nod. 'And yes, while I may, at times, borrow items without asking, that is **borrowing**, not stealing.'

I saw Mum raise an eyebrow, but she didn't say anything.

Edna joined the conversation. She leant forward and tapped the table with a stubby finger. 'Exchanging isn't stealing either,' she said. 'Especially if the thing you exchange it with looks exactly the same. Exchanging is exchanging.'

'That's right,' Grandma said firmly. 'Not that Edna and I have any plans to exchange anything in the near future. **Definitely not**. None at all.'

'None,' Edna agreed.

Thomas was looking bewildered. I wasn't surprised. I was finding it quite hard to keep up and I'm used to Grandma.

'Now where was I before Ollie interrupted?' Grandma said. 'Oh yes. Giving things back. I am going to give something back to society!'

Mum looked even more pleased. 'To society? Well, I think that's wonderful,' she said. 'They're looking for staff at the charity shop. You know. The one on the high street? You could do a few hours there? Sorting the clothes and dusting knick-knacks?'

'Volunteering is such a splendid thing to do,' Thomas said. 'Well done, you two.' He gave them a little clap.

'Oh, we're **not** volunteering.' Grandma tutted. 'Edna and I are doing something much more important. Something for the good of a whole nation.'

Blimey. I blinked. 'What?' I said.

'Can't tell you.' Edna looked triumphant.

We all looked at her. There were crumbs in her bristles.

'Why not?' I said.

She tapped the side of her nose. 'Because then you'd know.'

We all looked at Grandma. 'Know what?' I asked.

'Edna's right.' Grandma nodded. 'We can't tell you. **It's top secret**. If word of what we're about to do gets out, then ...' She drew her finger across her throat.

'You're so funny, Florence,' Mum said. 'I'll tell the man from the charity shop to get in touch.'

The doorbell rang.

'I'll get it,' Mum said, standing up. 'I'm expecti—' She stopped and looked surprised. 'Edna? Is everything all right?'

'Contact lens,' Edna said, from under the table. 'Dropped it. Don't mind me. You get on with answering the door.'

'Oh. OK. Ollie, help her look, will you?' Mum said.

She went out into the hall.

I slid off my chair and joined Edna under the table. She started to vigorously pat the carpet. I started patting the carpet too, though I wasn't quite sure what we were patting it for. 'What does it look like?' I asked.

'Small,' Edna said. **'Very small.'** She carried on patting.

Mum trotted back in with a small bunch of flowers.

'Anyone interesting, Sukey?' Grandma enquired casually.

'Mrs Briggs,' Mum said. 'From two doors down. She brought me these. I'm not sure why, but wasn't that kind of her?'

'Did you hear that, Edna?' Grandma raised her voice. **'Just a neighbour.'**

'Excellent,' said Edna, hoisting herself back on to her seat.

'Did you find it? Mum asked

'Yep.' Edna held her finger in the air. 'Here.'

She made a great show of tipping her head back and putting her lens back in. It must have been small – like she said – as I couldn't see it.

I'll tell you what I did see though, when she lifted up her arm and the sleeve of her duffel slid up slightly.

I saw something around her wrist. Something shiny.

Was Edna wearing handcuffs?

I **looked at** Edna. Then I looked at Grandma. I narrowed my eyes.

What was going on?

'Can I help you to a sandwich?' Thomas pushed the plate under my nose. 'They're cucumber.'

Mum had even cut the crusts off. 'No, thanks,' I said.

'I'll have one.' Edna's hand shot out.

'Make that your last,' Grandma said. 'We need to get going. Do our bit.'

'Absolutely.' Edna pushed a sandwich into her duffel pocket. Then she snapped open her handbag and stuffed some more in there. 'Can't wait.'

'Are you using the balloon?' Piper asked.

'Of course,' Grandma said. 'I left it on the Green. Thought it best, after last time. Didn't want to land on your onions again, Sukey.'

'Thank you, Florence,' Mum said. 'Very thoughtful.'

'When will you be back?' I asked.

'No idea,' Grandma said. 'We can't possibly put a timescale on something as **important** as the thing we're going to do.'

'That we can't tell you about.' Edna tapped her nose again.

'I'll just show Edna round your dad's workshop before we go.' Grandma picked up Rose. 'Such a shame we missed him. You wouldn't happen to know if he's got a **hacksaw**, would you?'

'Probably,' Mum said. 'I'll find you the key.'

I stared after them. What were they up to?

I decided to find out. I pushed my chair back and stood up.

'Careful,' Piper said.

OOPS.

Edna had left her handbag on the table and I caught it with my elbow.

I grabbed at it, but missed. If she hadn't crammed so many sandwiches into it, the catch might have stayed closed when it hit the floor. But no. It didn't. It **exploded** all over the place. **BUM.** Now I'd have to pick everything up. 'Would you like a hand, Ollie?' Thomas offered.

'Thanks,' I said. 'But no need.'

I knelt and started piling everything back in.

Edna had some odd stuff. As well as the sandwiches, there were two small tins of gold paint, a magnifying glass and something that looked like an eggcup.

Why would anyone have an **EGGCUP** in their handbag? I stared at it for a moment. **How strange**.

The back door slammed.

'Shall I help?' Piper peered under the table.

I shoved the eggcup back and snapped the catch shut. 'No,' I said. I stood up.

Phew. Just in time.

'Here you are, Edna.' I held it out.

'Ta.' She snatched it. 'Didn't look in it, did you?'

'No,' I said. 'Of course not.'

Piper raised an eyebrow.

Well, I hadn't!

Mum showed them to the door. 'Edna, you must come again. And it's been lovely to see you, Florence.'

'Yes, charming,' called Thomas, from the sink. 'Absolutely delightful.'

He couldn't mean that.

'Bye, Ollie's gran. Bye, Rose.' Piper kissed his nose.

'Bye, Grandma,' I called, as they went down the path. 'See you soon.'

'Maybe.' Grandma turned and drew her finger across her neck. **'Maybe not.'**

By the time we got back to the kitchen, Thomas had cleared the table and washed everything up.

Mum called him a sweetheart! Then she turned to me. 'Could you vacuum the rug, Ollie? Edna dropped a lot of crumbs and I need to get on with some work.'

Thomas put his hand up. 'I'll vacuum, Sukey.'

I'd have been more than happy to let him, but Mum said he'd already done quite enough, considering he was a guest.

I pulled the hoover out of the cupboard and started clattering about with it. **Some holiday this was!** First there was Thomas, sucking up all over the place, then Dad going away **again**, Grandma **retiring** – and now I had to do housework!

'Would you mind getting your enormous feet out of the way?' I said to Piper.

'You're being a right grump,' Piper said. '*Dancing*

with the Stars is on in a minute. Do you want to watch it?'

'Oh!' Thomas gave a little start. 'May I watch it with you, Piper? I do like dance, and there's no TV at school.'

'No TV?' Piper looked horrified. **'No TV at all?'**

'No,' Thomas said. 'If we have any spare time, we have to study. By the end of Year Six, we're expected to be fluent in eighteen languages.' He reeled off a list.

'Blimey,' Piper said. 'I haven't even heard of some of those. Say something in ... let me think ... Russian.'

Thomas blinked. 'I haven't revised for a while,' he said, 'but I'll give it a go.'

Just as he opened his mouth, I switched the hoover on. **HA.** I wasn't going to listen to him showing off.

Piper shouted over the noise. 'Ollie?'

'What?' I said. I vacuumed vigorously. She was going to have to ask pretty nicely if she wanted me to join them.

'If you're not going to watch, then when you've done that, could you bring us some biscuits?'

I turned the hoover up to max.

7

I'd sucked up almost all the crumbs when the brush hit something. Something small and heavy, that rolled across the room.

I caught a glimpse of it, sparkling in the light, before it disappeared under the dresser.

Eh?

I switched the hoover off and went over.

There wasn't much of a gap between the dresser and the floor, and it was dark under there – but I could just about see something glinting against the skirting board. Something round ... no. **Not round. Oval.**

I stretched out on my stomach and reached under.

'Has Myrtle escaped again?'

Piper had come to get the Jaffa Cakes.

I sat up and scowled at her. 'Nope.'

She put a whole one in her mouth. 'Why are you in such a bad mood?'

'Pardon?' I said. 'I can't hear you through the biscuit.'

'I don't know why you don't like Thomas,' she said. 'I think he's nice. **Are you jealous?**'

'Of what?'

'His school? All the puddings?'

Eh? What was she talking about? I wouldn't want to go to Thomas's school if they had a million puddings. Why would I want to live away from Mum and Dad and Myrtle, and learn eighteen languages and have no TV?

I couldn't think of anything worse.

Oh.

I suddenly felt quite sorry for Thomas.

I decided to try and be nicer.

'It's not him,' I said.

'What then?' Piper asked.

'It's Grandma,' I said. 'I can't believe she's going to

give up exploring.'

Just saying it made me feel sad.

'Don't worry,' Piper said. 'I'm first in the line for her balloon. We can do loads of fun stuff.'

'Balloons cost quite a lot, I think,' I said.

Piper shrugged. 'If I have to, I'll use my caravan money.'

I pointed out that she didn't have any caravan money yet.

'I will when we've found some treasure.' She knelt down next to me. 'If you're not looking for Myrtle, what are you doing?'

'Something went under.' I lay flat and reached out again. There was a lot of dust. Maybe if I mentioned it to Thomas he'd ... **Aha**. I had it. I rolled whatever it was towards me and pulled it out.

Oh.

Blimey.

I blinked.

It was an egg.

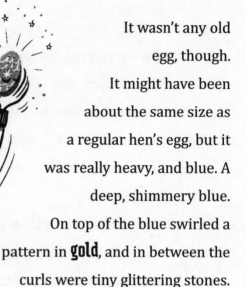

It wasn't any old
egg, though.
It might have been
about the same size as
a regular hen's egg, but it
was really heavy, and blue. A
deep, shimmery blue.
On top of the blue swirled a
pattern in **gold**, and in between the
curls were tiny glittering stones.

Most of them were pink, but every now and then
there was a yellow one, shaped like a star.

'Wow,' Piper said. 'That's **SO** pretty. Was it from
your Christmas tree?'

'No,' I said. 'I've never seen it before.'

Piper took it and held it up. 'Where do you think
it came from?'

I shrugged. 'Edna's bag, maybe?'

'The votes are in, Piper.' Thomas stuck his head
round the door. 'Are yo— Oh!'

I've never seen anyone's eyes pop out of their head before, but I **swear** his almost did.

'CRIKEY,' he said. 'Where did you get that from?'

'It was under the dresser.' Piper stood up. 'It's a Christmas decoration.'

Thomas shook his head. He took a step closer. 'No, it's not,' he said.

'Isn't it?' Piper said. 'It's ever so sparkly.'

Thomas reached out and took it from her. He held it up and turned it, slowly. 'Oh my,' he said. 'Oh my.'

'Oh my, what?' said Piper.

Thomas didn't reply. He just kept staring at the egg.

We waited for him to say something.

He didn't.

'Thomas?' Piper said. **'THOMAS?'**

He jumped. 'Sorry.' He looked quite stunned. 'It's the one that went missing. It's been missing for thirty years.'

'Eh?' I said.

Thomas took a deep breath. 'It's the **Moscow Star**.'

'Eh?' I said again.

'The Moscow Star.' He gazed at it in awe. '**The most valuable of all.**'

'The most valuable of all what?' Piper asked.

'Of all the Fabergé eggs.'

Eh? What on earth was he talking about? 'Fabby what?' I said.

'It's not fabby,' Thomas said. 'It's pronounced fab – er – jay. Gustav Fabergé was a jeweller. He made ornamental Easter eggs for the **Tsar of Russia**, over a hundred years ago.'

'Did he?' Piper said. 'Out of chocolate?'

'No.' Thomas shook his head. 'They used gold and the very finest gems. Each egg contained a magnificent surprise, and took over a year to make.'

'How do you know so much about them?' I stood up and went over for another look.

'I did my Year Five project on Fabergé's

work,' Thomas said.

'Oh yes,' I said. 'I remember your mum saying. You got an A.'

Thomas blushed. 'Something like that. This is definitely the Moscow Star.' He rotated it in his hand. 'Those stars are cut from diamonds, and if you press them in the right order, the egg opens.'

'Really?' I reached out and pushed one, then another. Nothing happened. 'What's inside?'

'No one knows for sure.' Thomas said. 'It's what makes this egg so special. There's a rumour it's an emerald. **An emerald the size of a pigeon's egg**. The Tsar tried to crack the combination for years, but never managed it. It's suspected the mechanism was faulty.'

'He should have kept the receipt,' I said. 'Mum always takes stuff back. You usually get twenty-eight days.'

'Let's drop it from the upstairs window.' Piper gave a little hop. 'That might sort it.'

Thomas clutched the egg to his chest. 'I think not, Piper,' he said. 'This egg is **priceless**.'

I looked at him. 'It not the real one,' I said. 'How can it be?'

Thomas looked stubborn. 'I'm sure it is,' he said.

'I know!' Piper dashed to the door. 'The metal detector! We'll put it on the Gold and Silver setting.'

Thomas gasped. 'What a **fabulous** idea!' He turned to me. 'Oh. Can you imagine if we've found it, Ollie? After all these years.'

'Here it is.' Piper came back in. 'Don't forget, Ollie, we agreed a fifty-fifty split on any treasure.'

'On stuff we dug up,' I said. 'Not stuff that was under my dresser.'

'That wasn't in the small print.' Piper switched on the detector. 'Put the egg on the floor, Thomas.'

'We should make sure that it works first.' Thomas sounded anxious. 'We don't want a false negative.' He looked around. 'Have you got something we can use for a test, Ollie? A silver dish? A gold statuette?'

I stared at him. 'Of course, Thomas,' I said. 'Our house is full of things like that. Let me go and fetch my box of doubloons.'

Piper giggled. 'Come on, Ollie,' she said. 'Your mum must have some earrings?'

I went and had a look. Mum did have some that looked quite fancy. I brought them down.

'Put them under the rug,' Piper said. 'I'll turn my back so I don't know where they are.'

'OK.' I pushed them under. 'Done.'

Piper swung the detector.

It beeped.

'Yay!' Piper clapped. 'It works!'

'Now for the egg.' Thomas reverently placed it in position.

Piper swung the detector.

It beeped.

OMG!

We all looked at each other.

No.

The egg couldn't be real, could it?

'Hang on,' said Piper. 'We forgot to move the earrings.' She fished around under the rug and pulled them out. 'Let's have another go.'

The egg lay there, in all its glory.

Piper waved the detector.

Then she did it again.

It didn't beep.

She swept it across for a third time.

NOTHING.

Thomas looked devastated. 'You were right, Ollie,' he said. '**It's a fake.**'

'Told you,' I said.

I didn't let Thomas see, but I was almost as disappointed as he was. I'd never really thought it was the missing egg, but it would have been brilliant if it had been.

'Oh well,' Piper said. 'I guess it's back to Plan A. Ollie and I are going treasure hunting tomorrow, Thomas. Do you want to come and help?'

He beamed at her. 'I would be delighted,' he said. 'I can most certainly advise you on the best places to dig.'

Plan A wasn't going to happen either. Mum had other ideas. She told us about them over breakfast.

'I've booked you a punt,' she said. 'I thought you could have a lovely day on the river. Though I've just discovered they don't supply life jackets, so I'm having second thoughts.'

'I've got my lifesaver's badge,' Thomas said.

'Of course you have.' Mum looked relieved. 'Your mum told me. Acquired last winter off the coast of Iceland in stormy seas, wasn't it?'

Thomas opened his mouth to say something, but Mum was still talking. 'I'm afraid I can't come with you,' she said. 'I've got to go into work. Something's come up. A paving emergency.'

'Don't worry,' I said. 'We'll be fine by ourselves.'

'Oh no, Ollie.' Mum shook her head. 'I called

Grandma Beatrix. She's going to take you.'

Grandma Boring? Great.

Thomas beamed at Mum across the table. 'It's very good of you to arrange it for us,' he said. 'And can I just say this homemade muesli is delicious. Could you possibly let me have the recipe?'

'Of course.' Mum looked thrilled. 'I'll write it down for you.'

I stabbed my toast with the butter knife. Being nice to Thomas was hard. 'Did you invite Piper?' I asked.

'Yes,' said Mum, 'I called her mum last night to go through the risk assessment. I thought about asking her to fill out a permission slip bu—'

'Mum,' I said. 'It's **punting**.'

'That's what she said. She was quite sharp. I got the impression she was tired out with the babies. It must be terribly busy in that house.'

'It is.' Piper stuck her head round the door. 'I didn't think I'd make it. I had to get my brothers up extra early to give them breakfast. You should have heard the moaning.'

'Did you manage to eat, Piper?' Mum said. 'Would you like some muesli?' She shook the Tupperware tub. 'It's very nutritious. Tempted?'

'Thanks, Ollie's mum, but I had chocolate spread on toast.'

Mum shuddered. Personally, **I would kill** for chocolate spread on toast, but apparently, it's not *high-fibre* enough.

'I must go.' Mum stood up and grabbed her bag. 'Grandma Beatrix should be here any minute. The tickets are by the printer. I packed you a picnic; it's in the fridge. Have a nice time.'

'We will,' said Piper. 'Bye.'

Thomas looked at the clock. He put his spoon down. 'It's almost nine thirty,' he said. 'Shall we depart?'

'No rush, Thomas,' I said. 'Finish your breakfast.'

Piper went over to the dresser and picked

up Edna's egg, which we'd left in a teacup. She looked at it sadly. 'It's such a shame it's a copy,' she said. 'I googled it last night. The real one vanished from a museum in St Petersburg, thirty years ago. No one knows—'

She stopped. 'What's that noise?' she said.

'Eh?' I listened.

There was a noise. Outside. A roaring noise. Followed by a whistling.

Followed by a crash.

'GRANDMA!'

Piper and I raced to the back door. I flung it open.

YAY! There she was, scrambling out of the balloon basket.

Blimey, what was she wearing? I'd seen her yeti coat before, but not that **enormous furry hat**. Rose had a coat on too, and some little bootees, which looked very much like the ones Mum had knitted for Piper's baby sisters.

We ran over.

'Here. Take Rose.' Grandma passed him to Piper.

'We weren't expecting you,' I said. 'We were expecting Grandma Beatrix.'

'She couldn't make it. She asked me to come instead.'

I looked at her. That didn't sound very likely. 'Really?' I said.

'Yes. I phoned to tell her about the squirrel. She doesn't like squirrels.'

'Squirrel?' Piper said. 'What squirrel?'

Grandma ignored her. 'I'd have been here sooner, but I thought your mum would never go. I hope she doesn't mind too much about her pots.' She looked around at the mess. 'What a silly place to leave them, right there on the patio.'

'Why are you back?' I asked. 'Where's Edna?'

'Edna?'

'Yes,' I said. 'Edna.'

Grandma snorted. 'Prison.'

'Prison?' Piper's mouth fell open. 'What happened?'

'I'll tell you inside. Come on.'

I made Grandma a cup of tea (in a mug, like regular people) and got out Mum's biscuits.

Edna's egg sat twinkling in the sugar bowl. Once Grandma had got over the shock of seeing it, she'd put it there for safekeeping.

Thomas raised his hand. 'Can I just ask, are we going punting, or not? Because,' he tapped his watch, 'we should really get going.'

Grandma shook her head. 'I'm afraid, Thomas, there'll be no punting today. A **rogue squirrel** is attacking the customers. They've had to shut.'

Thomas looked incredulous. 'Really?'

'I'd **never** lie,' Grandma said.

Piper picked up Rose and started unlacing his bootees. 'Come on, Ollie's gran,' she said. 'What happened to Edna?'

Grandma took a slurp of her tea. 'I'll need to be quick. Your mum could be back any minute.'

'We're listening,' I said.

'Well, just before Christmas, I visited **St Petersburg**. That's in Russia, Ollie.'

'I know where St Petersburg is,' I said.

'Quite by chance, I ended up in a museum. A museum dedicated to the work of one man. **The greatest jeweller in all of Russia.**'

'Fabergé?' Piper said.

'That's right, Piper!' Grandma looked impressed. 'How clever you are!'

'Thomas told her, actually,' I said.

'Whatever.' Grandma stuffed a whole custard cream into her mouth. 'Fabergé made Easter eggs. I mean, when I saw that in the guidebook, my first thought was of chocolate! I only popped in because I thought there might be samples. I was very disappointed. I almost left immediately, but the guide suggested I take a look.' She went a bit misty-eyed. 'Oh, the eggs were beautiful, Piper. Exquisite. I could have gazed at them for ever.'

'Well, this one's amazing.' Piper rolled it around in the sugar. 'And it's not even real.'

Grandma went on. 'While I was there I got talking to **Viktor**, the curator. A delightful man ... very ... Russian. Just about to retire. He's overseen the eggs for fifty years!'

'He must be ancient,' I said.

Grandma frowned. 'Distinguished, Ollie. Distinguished. Anyway. He told me all about the Moscow Star, and why it was so highly prized.'

'I know.' Thomas put his hand up. 'It wouldn't open. No one knew what was inside.'

'Exactly right, Thomas.' Grandma applauded. 'A simple mechanical fault rendered it priceless. Anyway. **It was stolen**. One spring evening. Viktor was on holiday.'

'How did the thieves get in?' I asked.

'Through the back door. They must have picked the lock. They turned the electricity off to disable the alarm, and plucked the egg from its case.'

'Do they know who took it?' I asked.

'Viktor found the subject painful to talk about, so I made enquiries elsewhere.' Grandma pulled a notebook from her bag, and flipped it open. 'It seems the politsiya suspected a number of people. The first was **Count Nikolai Pavlov**. He said he was a reincarnation of the Tsar, and wanted his eggs back. He was evicted from the museum three days before the robbery, and vowed revenge.'

'Who else?' Piper asked.

'**Olga Kolovska**. An opera singer with a passion for rare jewels. She made no secret of her love for the Moscow Star. Shortly after the theft, she gave up performing and moved to Vladivostok.'

'Very suspicious,' Thomas said.

Grandma turned another page. 'The final suspect was a local billionaire, **Leo Bolonski**. He made his money from cheesy snacks. He'd visit the museum every day, gazing for hours at the eggs. He was obsessed by the Moscow Star. After the egg disappeared, Leo stopped coming.' She leant forward. 'It was him, I know it.'

'How?' I asked.

'Viktor reported a single cheesy snack lying crushed by the back door. Sadly, by the time the politsiya arrived, a pigeon had eaten it.'

'Was that the only evidence?' I asked.

'No.' Grandma leant forward and tapped the table. 'Leo also owned a **barometer**.'

'An instrument to predict the weather?' Thomas blinked.

'Yes.'

'What's that got to do with stealing an egg?' Piper asked.

'Don't you see?' Grandma thumped the table. 'Whoever took the egg knew what they were doing. They chose the night the snow thawed!'

'I still don't get it,' I said.

'In those days,' Grandma said, 'the politsiya relied on footprints in the snow. They'd follow them backwards from the scene of the crime, and, bingo. They'd have their man.'

Thomas stared at her. 'The police couldn't just have relied on footprints,' he said.

Grandma shrugged. 'It was **thirty years ago**. No one had heard of DNA. There wasn't any CCTV. They barely had telly, let alone *Crimestoppers*.' She gave a little sigh. 'Those were the days.'

'So the Moscow Star was never recovered?' I said.

'No.' Grandma shook her head. 'There wasn't enough proof, and also, Leo's aunt was the chief of the politsiya. She refused to consider he might be involved.'

'Ah,' Thomas said. 'I see.'

Grandma took out a tissue and dabbed her eye. 'There is never a moment that poor Viktor does not grieve the loss. He blames himself, you know, for taking a holiday.' She clasped her hands. 'I wanted to help, but I didn't know how. I said goodbye and flew home, but all the while I was thinking of his sad little face. I needed a plan.'

'So you bought him a fake egg?' I looked at it, sitting there in the sugar bowl. 'To make up for the stolen one?'

'Of course not, Ollie.' Grandma tutted. 'That would be a rubbish plan. My plans are **never** rubbish.'

Piper giggled. 'Go on, Ollie's gran. I love your plans.'

'Thank you, Piper.' Grandma gave her a nod. 'Well, that night I happened to be scrolling through *Great Potton Online*, catching up on local news, when a headline caught my eye.' She held out her phone. 'Look.'

'**Blimey.**' I took the phone for a better look. 'Is that Edna?'

'Let me see.' Piper pushed me out the way. '**OMG.**' She looked at Grandma. '**Edna is a Master Forger?**'

I was really surprised. Edna hadn't looked like a master of much, to me.

'A criminal?' Thomas said. 'Gracious.'

Grandma shook her head. 'Edna is more artist than criminal, Thomas. She has a wonderful reputation. Artworks in all the major galleries.' She took a bite of biscuit. 'I mean, I'd heard of her, of course, but due to the nature of her work, she's always kept a low profile. I hadn't an inkling she'd been incarcerated at the Great Potton Correctional Facility for Lady Cons Over Fifty. Not until I read that.' She pointed at the phone in my hand. 'And that's when I had my idea!'

'Go on,' Piper said.

'I popped in to see her. We came to an agreement. I'd help her escape, and in return, she'd make me a copy of the Moscow Star, no questions asked.'

My mouth dropped open. I stared at the egg. **'Edna made that?'**

'Yes. I gave her a picture. As soon as she was out, we got everything we needed from Hobbies R Us.'

'Even the tiny little diamonds and rubies?' Piper raised her eyebrows.

'It's amazing what they sell, Piper.' Grandma waved a small packet of gems. 'She stuck them on with PVA.'

'The stuff we use at school?' I said.

Grandma nodded. 'I did think superglue would be a better option, but Edna was keen to come in under budget. Don't worry. It'll be fine as long as it doesn't get wet.'

I moved my glass of juice. I wasn't going to be held responsible for another glue-related incident.

Grandma went on. 'She did an **incredible** job. Just look at it. Such detail. She barely needed to look at the picture. You'd almost think she'd made one before.'

I still didn't get it. 'But why?' I asked. 'If it's not for Viktor, what are you going to do with it?'

Grandma tutted. 'Don't you see?' she said. 'I was going to track down the Moscow Star, and swap it for that.' She pointed at the egg in the sugar bowl. 'Edna was keen to get out of the country, so she offered to help.'

I stared at her. Was she serious? 'You were going to turn up at Leo Bolonski's, get him to produce a priceless egg he stole thirty years ago, then swap it for a fake?'

'Exactly.' Grandma beamed.

'But you don't even know Leo,' Piper said.

'I'm his cousin, actually.' Grandma looked nonchalant. 'On his father's side. Twice removed.'

I looked at her. 'No, you're not.'

She's such a liar.

Grandma took no notice. 'Leo was thrilled when I called. He was so fond of my mother – though strangely, he didn't remember me at all.'

'Gracious.' I said. 'What a surprise.'

'I felt quite hurt, Ollie.' Grandma dabbed her eye

again. 'Anyway. He couldn't wait to make amends, and invited Edna and I to dinner. It was all going swimmingly until we landed at the airfield just outside St Petersburg.'

Thomas had his hand up. 'Excuse me, Florence. Am I to understand you flew to Russia in your balloon?'

'That's right, Thomas. We did. Would you mind not interrupting?' Grandma gave him a frown.

'But how di—'

Grandma ignored him and carried on. 'As soon as we touched down, I popped off to the loo and left Edna to blag her way through customs. By the time I came out the politsiya had descended. Hundreds of them, in their little furry hats.'

'Why?' Piper asked.

Grandma snorted. 'Edna. No sooner had she handed over her passport than her face popped up on their little screen. They arrested her immediately.'

'For what?'

'The Great Potton Correctional Facility had put

her on an international "wanted" list.' Grandma munched dolefully on the last custard cream. 'I didn't realise she was that important.'

'What did you do?' I asked.

'I grabbed Rose, hopped into the balloon and headed back. I assumed the egg was in Edna's bag. I couldn't carry out the plan without it, could I?'

'You left Edna there?'

'I'm not proud, Ollie.' Grandma dabbed her eye. 'The politsiya are **scary**.'

'I can't believe she went all the way over there without the egg,' Piper said.

Grandma cheered up. 'I know! Isn't it wonderful?

Now we can have another go. I'll rearrange supper with Leo, and this time we'll bring the Moscow Star home. For Viktor, and the nation.' She gazed dreamily into the distance. 'Can you imagine his face, Piper? When he sees his precious egg has been returned?'

'Excuse me.' Thomas looked worried. 'The stealing sounds a bit risky – and possibly against the law?'

'You can't steal something that's already been stolen, Thomas.' Grandma nodded wisely. 'And in any case, it's swapping, which is not the same at all.' She looked around. 'Are there any more biscuits?'

'I'll go and see.' Thomas took the plate and went over to the cupboard.

'He's sort of right, though,' I said. 'Suppose you get caught?'

Piper giggled. 'Stop being such a **worrier**, Ollie. Your gran will have Rose with her. He'll be casting his lucky aura all over the place.'

'Exactly.' Grandma gave Rose a pat. 'What could possibly go wrong?'

I thought about the trifle.

'And Edna?' Piper asked.

'Edna?' Grandma looked surprised.

'You'll need to go and rescue her, won't you? So she can help you switch the egg?'

'Oh no.' Grandma said. 'I'll get her out afterwards – if there's time. Now. I'll need a quick word with your mum, Ollie, and then we'll get going.'

'We?' I blinked.

'Yes.' Grandma stood up. 'I'm taking you lot instead. Come on. **Get cracking.**'

I couldn't believe Grandma was taking us with her!
Woohoo!

'Oh **YAY**,' Piper said. She hopped up and down.
'That's ace, Ollie's gran. We won't let you down.'

I wondered what Grandma was going to tell Mum.
She's not generally keen on things that Grandma
suggests, even when they don't involve crossing the
continent in a hot-air balloon, and swapping stuff.

I looked over at Thomas, who was carefully
arranging party rings on a plate.

'What about him?'

'Oh, he has to come,' Grandma said. 'Definitely. We
may be thrown into all sorts of situations out there.
His skills will come in useful.'

'Tidying? Washing up?' I blinked. 'We're not going
to be doing any of that in Russia, are we?'

'He speaks Russian, Ollie,' Piper said.

'There you go then,' Grandma said. 'No question. He's coming.'

Did no one else find Thomas annoying?

He trotted over with the biscuits.

'We're going to St Petersburg, Thomas. You're coming with us,' Piper said. 'Is that OK?'

He looked delighted. 'Really?' he said. 'Gracious. I'd **love** that. Thanks for inviting me.'

'You don't have to,' I said, 'if you'd prefer to stay here.'

'Oh no. I never miss an opportunity to travel,' Thomas said. 'Especially somewhere as fabulous as Russia.'

'As long as you're up to it, Thomas?' Grandma took the plate and emptied it into her bag. 'Pretty manners are of no use if we go down in the Baltic and you have to **wrestle a shark**.'

'There aren't any sharks in the Baltic,' Piper said.

'I'd be more than happy to take one on,' Thomas

said. 'If there were.'

'That's the spirit.'
Grandma gave him a
whack on the back.

It looked like
Thomas was coming. I,
as usual, had not had
my opinion taken into
consideration.

I was so busy feeling
annoyed, I didn't notice Mum walking in.

She looked ever so surprised to see Grandma.

'What are you doing here?' she asked. 'Where's
Grandma Beatrix?'

'She couldn't make it.' Grandma grabbed the egg
from the sugar bowl and stuffed it into her bag. 'She
asked if I could come instead.'

'Really?' Mum raised her eyebrows. 'What about
your project? The way you were talking yesterday I
didn't think you'd be back for ages.'

'Our project is ongoing, Sukey. It will be a huge success. Thank you for asking.' Grandma gave her a nod.

'Was everything OK at work, Mum?' I asked.

'Yes. Someone phoned in a code red. An uneven paving slab outside the Post Office.' She shook her head. 'Honestly. I rushed all the way there, and it was as flat as a pancake!'

I looked suspiciously at Grandma.

Mum suddenly noticed the time. 'Shouldn't you three be on a punt by now?'

'The punting place is shut,' Thomas said. 'There's a squirrel attacking the customers.'

'That's right.' Grandma nodded. 'It was here earlier. It went completely **crazy**. Look what it did to your pots.'

Mum looked horrified. 'Oh my.' She grabbed her bag. 'I must get back to the office and despatch the dangerous mammal team.'

'One minute, Sukey,' Grandma said. She reached

into her pocket. 'Before you go.'

'What?' Mum said. She looked around. 'Has anyone seen my keys?'

Grandma brandished a piece of paper. 'A while back, Piper and Ollie, under my expert tutelage, wrote ... um ... a poem, and entered it into a competition!'

'Did we?' I didn't remember entering any competition.

'Yes, Ollie. You did.' Grandma waved the paper at Mum. **'They won!'**

Mum blinked. 'Congratulations, you two. What was the poem about?'

'Death,' Piper said, quickly. 'It was very dark. Poems always are.'

Grandma clutched the paper to her chest. 'The judges were terribly impressed. There's a wonderful prize.'

'What is it?' Mum said. She started pulling her coat back on.

'An invitation to a conference for the gifted and

talented. Three inspiring days of analytical discussion and debate. Thomas is invited too.'

Thomas clapped his hands. 'Oh, wonderful,' he said. 'I love to debate. I hope it doesn't clash with our trip to Russ— OW.'

I stepped off his foot. 'Sorry,' I said.

'Well, that sounds worthwhile, Florence.' Mum started to head for the door. 'When is it?'

'It starts this afternoon,' Grandma said. 'Don't you worry, Sukey. I know you've got stuff on, so I'll get them there.'

'Would you mind?' Mum looked relieved. 'That would be incredibly helpful. The squirrel thing will probably keep me busy all week.'

11

We waited till Mum had gone around the corner, and then went to pack. Grandma had said not to bring much, so Thomas got told off when he came down with three suitcases and a huge bag of toiletries.

'We are not emigrating, Thomas,' she huffed. 'Russia is practically down the road. You only need a jumper – and, if you absolutely must, a toothbrush.'

'Does anyone want a hat?' I asked. I had about a **million** that Mum had knitted for me. Thomas said he'd like one so I gave him the itchiest.

Rose ran about getting in everyone's way, as usual.

Thomas kept sneezing. 'Is Rose coming?' he said.

'Of course.' Grandma walked past on her way to the balloon. 'Egg exchanging is a perilous business, Thomas.'

Thomas waited till she was out of earshot. 'She

doesn't **really** believe Rose is lucky, does she?'

'Why?' I said. 'Don't you?'

Thomas looked down at Rose, who'd stopped to have a vigorous scratch. 'Well, I've never come across a ... what was it? A **Dog of Destiny** before. How does he work?

I shrugged. 'No one's sure. Things just turn out better when he's around. Especially if he's awake.'

'And that's it?' Thomas looked bewildered. 'But how do you know which bits are down to Rose, and which would have happened anyway?'

'You don't,' I said. 'The line is quite blurry.'

Thomas opened his mouth to say something else, but Piper came over.

'I've got the picnic,' she said. 'And the metal detector. I expect Russia is full of buried treasure.'

'They're not pirates,' I said.

'No, but they had a revolution,' Piper said. 'I bet people dropped things when they were running away.'

'Maybe,' I said. 'Where is the egg, by the way?'

'It's here.' She pulled it out of her pocket. 'Your gran told me to find a safe place for it. **It mustn't get wet.**'

'Can someone untie the mooring ropes?' Grandma called from outside. 'We take off in five.'

Thomas couldn't wait to climb up the rope ladder, but as soon as we were in the basket, he started to look nervous.

'There's a hole in the floor,' he said. **'Why is there a hole in the floor?'**

'A rhino stepped on it,' I said. 'It's OK. I'll stuff it with a duvet.'

'No need to worry, Thomas,' Grandma said. 'It's perfectly safe. And even if it wasn't, we have Rose to protect us.'

Thomas didn't seem convinced. I swear he was looking around for a seatbelt.

'Right.' Grandma pulled open a hatch. 'Hold on.'

'Oooh.' Thomas suddenly forgot his nerves. 'Is that the engine?' he said. 'Ollie told me about it. I'd **LOVE** to have a peek.'

'Of course.' Grandma looked delighted. 'So lovely to have interest. It runs on distilled peanut oil. The engine sucks in air through these pipes here …' She pointed. 'And shoots it out over there. Like a jet.'

'Gracious.' Thomas blinked. 'One would hardly think it possible.'

I tried to work out if he was really interested, or sucking up as usual.

'And over here,' Grandma gestured, 'is the sat nav.

I've typed in the coordinates. We're all set. We'll be there at a quarter past six, Russian time.'

'Tomorrow evening?' Thomas eyes popped. 'That soon?'

'Tomorrow evening?' Grandma pulled on the burner. 'Oh no. This balloon is much better than that. A quarter past six, tomorrow morning.'

'Blimey,' said Thomas.

The balloon gave a lurch.

We were off.

Thomas found the whole 'engine' thing bewildering. 'But we're going so **fast**,' he kept shouting. His hair was whipping everywhere. 'The basket isn't streamlined. I don't understand how it works.'

'No one knows how bumblebees fly, either.' I jumped down into the bottom of the basket, out of the wind. 'But they do.'

'Shall we play a game?' Piper said. 'We've got ages.'

Thomas dropped down beside us. 'What a splendid idea,' he said. 'Have you got any cards?'

'I forgot to pack any,' I said.

'We could play **Truth or Dare**,' said Piper

'I've never played,' Thomas said. 'What are the rules?'

'We take it in turns to ask questions,' Piper

said. 'If you don't want to answer, you have to do a dare instead.'

'Oooh! I love this game.' Grandma abandoned the engine and pushed in next to me. 'Ask me first. **Go on!** Ask me anything.'

'OK.' I thought about it. 'Did you know those doughnuts weren't free samples?'

'Absolutely not!' Grandma huffed. 'What a question.'

She's **such** a liar.

'My turn to ask.' Grandma looked around. 'Let me think. OK. Here's one for Ollie.'

I was ready.

'Do you cheat at Monopoly?' She gave me a hard stare.

'No,' I said. 'I always win because I'm really good at it.' I gave her a hard stare back.

'There's no point playing if everyone's going to lie,' Piper said, crossly. She turned to Thomas. 'OK. If you could be anything at all in the world, what would you like to be?'

'Oh.' Thomas looked surprised. 'Well, Mum wants me to be **Prime Minister**.'

'No,' Piper said. 'What do you **WANT** to be? Anything at all. Like ... like a train driver. Or in charge of the pick and mix at Great Potton Pictures. Something you probably won't be, but would like to be.'

'Oh.' Thomas went a bit pink. 'I think I'll take a dare.'

'Don't be silly, Thomas.' Grandma gave him a pat. 'You're among friends.'

'I'll tell you what **I'd** like to be,' Piper said.

'What?' I said.

'I'd love to be a gymnast,' Piper said. 'You know. The ones with the hoops and balls.'

'Really?' I blinked. 'You're, like, the **least graceful** person I know.'

Piper looked cross. 'I didn't say I was going to be, did I? It would have been nice, that's all.' She looked at Thomas. 'Go on. Your turn. We won't laugh.'

'All right then.' Thomas tried to look nonchalant. 'I'd be a dancer.'

I blinked. **A dancer?** Blimey. I looked at him. So that's why he wanted to watch *Dancing with the Stars*. I would never have thought it of Thomas, if he hadn't said. He wasn't very lithe.

Piper was surprised too. 'Really?' she said. 'Like ballet?'

'Oh, I **love** the ballet,' said Grandma dreamily.

'I do like ballet,' Thomas said. 'But I prefer contemporary dance.'

'What's that?' I said.

'It's all about emotion, and feelings. It's dramatic.'

Grandma pulled a face. 'Oh, modern stuff. I've seen that. Lots of running about with scarves. There's always scarves. Why is tha— Oh.' She jumped up. 'You carry on playing. I need to adjust the rudder.'

'Have you ever done any contemporary dance, then?' Piper asked.

'I used to practise in my room.' Thomas's face fell. 'But the others kept videoing me and putting it on YouTube.'

'That's horrible,' Piper said.

'I know,' Thomas said, in a tiny voice. 'Everything at school is horrible.'

I looked at him in horror. He wasn't going to cry, was he?

He was.

His eyes had gone all shiny and as I watched, a tear welled up and rolled down his cheek. 'I **hate** it,' he said. 'Everyone expects me to be good at everything. The school expect it, and

my parents expect it, and I'm not.'

Blimey. This was awkward. I patted his shoulder. 'Yes, you are,' I said. 'Your mum says you're top in almost everything.'

He shook his head. 'I'm top in pottery. I'm in catch-up classes for everything else. I'm barely on level one in Russian.' He gave a big sob. 'I only do things for people so they like me. I'm the loser in "Only Losers Lose".'

'Thomas.' Piper patted his other shoulder. 'You're not a loser.'

'You know all about Fabergé,' I said. 'You got an A for your project.'

'I downloaded it from the Internet,' Thomas howled.

'We all do that,' Piper said. 'Some more than most.' She had the cheek to look at me!

'You need to focus on your strengths,' I said.

'I haven't got any.' Thomas covered his face and bawled.

'Yes you have.' I thought hard. 'You've got amazing manners.'

'And really nice hair,' Piper said.

'Have I?' Thomas brightened. 'I wasn't sure if I should get it cut or not.'

'Leave it,' Piper said. 'I like it as it is.'

'I'm back.' Grandma plonked herself back down. 'Whose go?'

'I think we're done,' I said. I didn't want to unleash any more of Thomas's emotions.

'Shall we have the picnic?' Piper suggested. 'I mean, there's nothing very tasty in it, mainly lentil bars and hard-boiled eggs, but I think I saw some flapjack.'

'There's definitely no flapjack.' Grandma brushed crumbs off her top. 'I checked. And I got rid of the eggs. Nasty smelly things. I chucked them over the side.'

'The ones in the tub?' Piper jumped up.

Grandma gave a nod. 'Eggs are banned from my balloon, Piper.'

Piper looked horrified. She put her face in her hands.

Eh? She didn't like hard-boiled eggs that much, did she?

'What's wrong?' I asked.

She shook her head. 'I can't tell you.'

'I told you about my dancing,' Thomas said encouragingly.

Piper looked at us through her fingers. 'It's too awful.'

'What is?'

'Edna's egg.'

'What about it?' I asked.

'It was in there.'

I stared at her, aghast. 'In the tub?'

'Edna's egg?' Grandma shrieked. She jumped to her feet. **'WHAT WERE YOU THINKING?'**

'You said not to get it wet! It was a plastic box! I thought it would be safe.'

'Hang on.' Grandma pulled the duvet out of the

hole in the floor and peered through. 'Nope. We're over the Baltic.' She stuffed the duvet back. 'Dry land would have been a different matter.' She flopped back down beside us. 'What were you thinking, Piper?'

'Don't blame me.' Piper sounded indignant. 'How was I supposed to know you'd go and do that?'

I suggested hanging out of the hole to look for it but Grandma shook her head.

'The water would have dissolved the glue by now.'

'I can't believe it,' Piper said, mournfully. 'I know it wasn't real, but it was so beautiful. I should have kept it in my pocket.'

'What bad luck.' Thomas looked glum.

'Where is Rose?' Grandma looked around.

'Under that blanket.' I pointed. 'Snoring.'

'HA.' Grandma looked triumphant. 'He can't cast his lucky aura when he's asleep. If he'd been awake, I would never have accidentally knocked the eggs over the side.'

'You said you threw them over,' I pointed out.

'By accident,' Grandma said. 'There you go, Piper. It was Rose's fault. No need to keep blaming yourself.'

Piper raised her eyebrows. 'Thanks,' she said. 'I won't.'

'So what now?' I said.

I really didn't want to go home.

Grandma leant over and pressed a switch. The balloon picked up speed. 'We'll rescue Edna. She'll have to make us another one.'

13

The closer we got to Russia the colder it got. I huddled under a duvet with Piper and Thomas until Grandma said we were almost there.

I got up and peered over the edge. We seemed to be coming down through a layer of cloud, because I couldn't see anything. Just white.

'Prepare for landing,' Grandma shouted.

'I'll get my passport.' Thomas reached for his bag. 'Where are the rest of the papers, Florence? Shall I get them out?'

'Papers?' Grandma looked confused.

'Yes. You know. The visas. All the official documents.'

'Oh.' Grandma gave a little laugh. 'Don't be silly, Thomas. We don't need anything like that.'

Thomas looked surprised. 'We don't?'

'They've changed the rules, Thomas. If you're travelling in a balloon, they let you fly straight in.'

'Really?'

'Absolutely.' Grandma nodded. 'I phoned to check, and they said that as long as we stay under the radar, we're welcome.'

'Oh.' Thomas looked at her, doubtfully. 'OK.'

'Where are we going to land?' I asked.

Grandma peered over the edge of the basket. 'Right here,' she said.

'Whoa!' shrieked Piper. We all pitched sideways.

I took my elbow out of Thomas's ear. Then I scrambled to my feet and hung over the side of the basket.

We were on a rooftop. A flat one.

Beyond it a whole city spread out.

Wow.

Snow.

I'd never seen anything so amazing. Everything sparkled.

St Petersburg was **nothing** like Great Potton.

The buildings were old. And grand. They had turrets! And domes! **Golden domes!**

Piper climbed up beside me.

She didn't say anything.

We just stood there looking at it.

It was so quiet and stil—

'I can't believe we got here so quickly.' Thomas jumped up next to us. 'It's totally 𝖋𝖆𝖇𝖚𝖑𝖔𝖚𝖘, isn't it? I came here on a school trip. We went to the ballet. The Russians are ever so good at ballet. They're good at all types of dance, in fact.'

'They're very **passionate** people, Thomas. That's why.' Grandma tucked Rose inside her coat and climbed out of the basket. 'You'll see when you meet Viktor. Careful not to slip. I wouldn't want to tell Sukey someone had plummeted off the edge.'

We followed Grandma on to the ice. The snow had been cleared from most of the roof, but it was still perilous.

Grandma passed me the mooring rope. 'Tie us up,' she said. 'There's a post over there. **Use a proper knot.** We don't want the balloon blowing away in a blizzard.'

Thomas tried to give me some advice, but I've learnt all about knots at Scouts so I didn't take any notice. I wasn't quite sure which I should use in this situation, but I did a pretty good job. No one would get that undone in a hurry!

'Where actually are we?' Piper asked Grandma.

'The museum. I called Viktor earlier, to say we'd be popping in. He was absolutely delighted to hear from me again.' She started to cross the roof. 'This way. Remember not to mention our plan. It's to be a surprise.'

'Is that the plan to switch an egg with an egg we haven't got?' muttered Piper.

'That's the one,' I said. 'Should we bring the bags?'

'OK.' Piper reached back in for them. 'What about the metal detector?'

'May as well.' I took it.

'Look.' Thomas pointed. 'See that building there, the white one? That's the St Petersburg School of Dance. They put on **wonderful** shows.' He skipped to catch up with Grandma. 'Do you think we might purchase some tickets whilst we're here, Florence?'

Blimey. Thomas had certainly stopped being embarrassed about his hobby. He'd be doing the polka in a minute.

Grandma stopped and waited. 'Here we are,' she said. She pointed down a single flight of stairs at a metal door. 'Through there.'

'I saw the handle turn,' Piper said. 'Someone's coming out.'

'Wonderful.' Grandma clopped down the steps. 'Our arrival has been noted.'

A figure appeared, silhouetted against the light behind.

I gulped and took a step back. Was that Viktor?

He was enormous.

His shoulders were the width of the doorframe. He was even taller than Grandma! He was swathed in furs so I couldn't see much of his face – but he had a remarkably long nose which jutted out from under his hat.

'Wow,' whispered Piper, from behind me. 'Scary.'

'**Viktor.**' Grandma held out her arms. 'We arrived! It was so kind of you to let us land on your roof.'

'Your balloon is **spectacular**. So incredibly fast.' Viktor's teeth glinted in the sun. 'Come in, out of the cold.'

Was that a smile? It was hard to tell.

We followed Grandma down the rest of the steps, and Viktor held the door for us to pass through.

Then he shut and bolted it, and turned to face us.

It wasn't all fur. **He also had a very big beard.**

He took Grandma's hand and kissed it. 'Florence,' he said. 'So **vonderful** to have you back.'

Grandma blushed. 'Lovely to see you, too, Viktor.' She pulled me forward. 'This is Ollie, my grandson.'

Viktor didn't look that pleased to see me, to be honest.

'Good morning.' He gave a little bow. 'Vot a pleasure.'

I don't think it was.

'Hi,' I said. 'This is Piper.'

'Nice to meet you,' Piper said. She gave Thomas a push. 'Thomas speaks Russian, Viktor.'

'Is that so?' Viktor raised his eyebrows.

Thomas nervously held out his hand. 'Хочу есть,' he said. 'Я хотел бы бутерброд с сыром.'

Viktor looked rather surprised. 'I'm not sure I have any cheese,' he said. He ignored Thomas's hand and turned back to Grandma.

Piper gave Thomas a nudge. 'What did you say?' she whispered.

'I thought I said I was pleased to meet him,' Thomas whispered back. 'But I could have been asking for a sandwich. They're on the same page. Sometimes I get mixed up.'

Honestly. I thought we'd only brought Thomas for his language skills.

Grandma was chatting away to Viktor. 'I hope you didn't mind us inviting ourselves,' she said. 'But I was right in the middle of some charitable works when there was a misunderstanding at the border. They arrested a friend of mine.'

'I heard,' Viktor said. 'I vos worried for you.'

'You heard?' Grandma looked surprised.

Viktor nodded. 'St Petersburg is small. News travels fast. When they said a criminal of note had been apprehended, and a lady had scarpered in a balloon, I vondered if it might be you.'

'I did not scarper.' Grandma sounded indignant. 'I went to gather reinforcements.'

'Of course.' Viktor smirked. 'And now you are back. You would **neffer** let your friend rot in jail.'

'Exactly,' Grandma said. 'She is **completely** innocent.'

'Innocent?' Viktor sucked his teeth. 'Our politsiya do not lock people away for nothing.'

'Mistaken identity,' Grandma said, firmly. 'That's what it was. Edna never forged anything.'

'Edna?' Viktor took a step back. 'Edna?' He stared at Grandma. 'Zat is an unusual name.' His nose quivered. 'You could not possibly be talking about

Edna McAngelo? **The greatest "replicator" the world has ever known?'**

He seemed strangely excited.

'Maybe.' Grandma looked shifty. 'Do you know her?'

Viktor nodded. 'She did some work for me, here in ze museum. Many, many years ago.' He clasped his hands. 'A vonderful woman. So warm.'

Grandma looked quite put out. 'If you say so,' she said. 'I find her a little gruff.'

Viktor gave himself a shake. 'Who vud have thought?' he said. 'After all these years. **Edna.**' He rubbed his hands. **'Vot perfect timing.'**

'Perfect timing?' Grandma blinked. 'What do you mean, perfect timing?'

'Ah,' Viktor said, quickly. 'Vot I mean is – zey vill be keeping her in the St Petersburg Reformatory. It is where they put ze prisoners before trial. It is just a couple of streets away.' He patted Grandma on the shoulder. 'It vill make it easy for you to visit.'

'Wonderful,' Grandma said. 'We'll head down there, as soon as we've had breakfast.'

'I hope you can secure her release,' Viktor said. 'Eet is a **terrible** jail. There is no heating. There are rats. Ze cook left last weekend. The prisoners have to gnaw on raw beetroot.'

'Beetroot?' Grandma looked aghast. 'Isn't that a vegetable?'

Viktor nodded. 'It is unhappy indeed. They advertise in ze paper but no vun cares to work with the convicts.' He spun around. 'Come. Zis way.'

We followed Viktor down another set of stairs and through two lots of fire doors. He padlocked them both behind us.

'Security,' muttered Grandma. 'Can't be too careful. Villains all over the place.'

We were in a small, dark passage. Viktor strode ahead, and then he stopped and unlocked another set of doors. Wooden ones this time.

He flung them open.

'My vonderful museum.'

Wow.

I stood and stared.

'Blimey,' said Piper.

'Do you like it?' said Thomas. 'It's **marvellous**, isn't it? It used to be a palace.'

I could tell. The corridor in front of us was the longest I'd ever seen. And the grandest. I looked up. **Oh my**. Just look at the ceiling. I'd never seen anything like it! It was painted all over with ladies and fat little babies and overflowing baskets of fruit. Huge marble columns held it up – and between them, great chandeliers sparkled like stars.

It was nothing like the museum in Great Potton, I'll tell you that much. Their ceiling was beige.

14

'**Gracious.**' **Grandma trotted** through the doorway after Viktor. 'I just love this carpet. Your feet really sink into it.'

Piper looked around in awe. 'The walls are covered in **velvet**, Ollie,' she said. 'I wouldn't want to bring the twins in here.'

Viktor was walking fast and it was a struggle to keep up, let alone look properly at anything. We hurried past statues and suits of armour and huge vases on plinths. The chandeliers glittered above. I started to sweat. It was boiling. Viktor's heating bills must be massive.

I pulled off my hat and started to shed layers. Where were we going?

Viktor swung right and pushed open another door. This one was quite normal sized, and he had quite a bit of trouble squeezing through it with all the furs on. Grandma gave him a helpful push.

'Many thanks.' He picked himself up from the floor. 'Do come in.' He gestured. 'Zis is my office.'

His office wasn't nearly as grand as the corridor. It was still big, but there was no painted ceiling and in the middle of it there was a desk with loads of stuff all over it, and some uncomfortable-looking chairs that didn't match.

Viktor removed his hat and put it on a shelf with several others. It was a unnecessarily big hat, I thought. Underneath it, his head was tiny, and completely bald.

'Let me take your cloak.' Grandma hung it on a peg for him.

Blimey ... what was he wearing? Were those pantaloons? And that wasn't a regular shirt, it was more of an open-necked blouse, with huge sleeves and embroidery on the cuffs. Over that was a knitted waistcoat.

I could see Thomas admiring it.

Grandma plonked herself down on one of the chairs. 'I've been telling Ollie about your museum,' she said. 'He couldn't wait to see St Petersburg for himself. The sights, the art, the food. Especially the food. He's so adventurous. He wants to immerse himself completely.'

Viktor looked at me and his mouth puckered. 'I do not generally like ze children,' he said. 'Children are sticky. Their faces are sticky, their hands are sticky. They peer through ze glass at my beautiful objects, and when they leave,' he gave me a fearsome glare, **'their stickiness remains.'**

Blimey.

'I blame the parents, Viktor,' Grandma commiserated.

'I too.' Viktor nodded. 'I'm forever in there with a duster. Honestly. **It never ends**.'

Eh? What had happened to his accent?

Piper stared at him. 'Are you sure you're Russian?'

she said. 'Just then, you sounded like one of my aunts.'

'Oh.' Viktor looked annoyed with himself. 'In my heart,' he put his hand on his chest and gave a little bow, 'I'm Russian, through and through. That's what counts.'

'So you're not, then?' Piper persevered.

Viktor glared at her. 'In my heart—'

'Where are you from?' Piper wasn't giving up.

Viktor flushed. **'Basildon.'**

'Basildon?' Thomas blinked. 'You're from Basildon? **In Essex?'**

'Yes.' Viktor scowled. Then he pulled off his beard and put it up by his hat. **Eh?**

We all stared at him.

'Tourists,' Viktor explained. 'They think all Russians have beards. It's what they expect.'

'Oh,' Piper said. 'Right.'

Grandma looked appalled. **'So you're not Russian? Not even a little bit?'**

Viktor flushed. 'No.'

'Well, you should have said!' Grandma was outraged. 'I'm not a tourist! I'm **very disappointed** in you, Viktor.'

'Sorry.' Viktor looked sulky.

'How long have you been in Russia?' Grandma asked.

'Ages.' Viktor walked over to his desk and picked up a photograph. He held it out. 'My seventh birthday party,' he said. 'Just before we left for St Petersberg.'

Grandma peered over and sniffed. 'Very English,' she said.

Viktor carried on. 'My parents were admirers of Fabergé. They came to work as caretakers, but the pay was rubbish. We were very poor. My friends all had ponies and summers by the sea – but I did not.'

'No pony? How terrible for you,' muttered Grandma.

Viktor nodded. 'It was. But over the years I came to appreciate the eggs.' He gave a little giggle. 'You must not feel sorry for me. What finer toys could a boy ask for?'

'I suppose you are very dedicated,' Grandma admitted grudgingly.

'I am.' Viktor nodded. 'When my parents retired, I was offered the job of curator. Since then I have devoted my life to this place. Well.' He paused. 'Apart from when I'm on holiday. I do like a good holiday. Somewhere hot.'

I turned the photo over. Next to the date was a name. 'Who's Steve?' I said.

Viktor blushed.

'Steve?' Grandma looked horrified. '**<u>STEVE?</u>**'

'It didn't go with the blouse,' Viktor mumbled. 'No one calls me that any more.'

Not much would go with that blouse, if you asked me.

'So. You're **not** Russian, and your real name is **Steve**,'

Piper said. 'Anything **else** we should know?'

Viktor brightened. 'I have some snacks.' He gestured towards a table at the side of the room. 'I got them especially.'

'Oh. How kind.' Grandma looked a little more forgiving. She peered over. 'They look delightful. Make sure you leave me some, Ollie. Rose needs to do his business. I shouldn't be too long.'

'Let me escort you,' Viktor said. He grabbed his hat and beard. 'I can point out the prison.'

Once they'd gone, I wandered over to the table to see what was on offer. There wasn't much. Just some little squares of toast, with jam on them.

'Ooh, lovely.' Thomas picked up the plate and offered it to me.

'No, thanks,' I said. It looked like blackcurrant jam, which isn't my favourite.

Thomas took one and popped it in his mouth. 'Delicious,' he said. 'Are you sure?'

I was quite hungry. I decided I could get over the blackcurrant. I picked one up and took a bite.

Eh?

There was something wrong with the jam.

Something **really** wrong.

Had it been poisoned?

My eyes bulged. What should I do? I looked around

for somewhere to spit it out. That vase would do. It didn't look priceless.

Thomas watched in surprise. 'Didn't you like it?' he said. 'Piper?' He offered her the plate. 'One for you?'

'No,' I croaked. Was I perspiring? Perspiring was definitely a symptom of poisoning. I'd read it in a book. **'Don't!'**

'Why?' Piper reached out to take one.

I smacked the tray out of Thomas's hands.

'Poison,' I croaked. 'The jam's poisoned.'

They stared at me.

'It's not jam. It's **caviar**.' Thomas looked bewildered. 'A Russian delicacy.'

'Caviar?' I stared at him blankly.

'Fish eggs,' Thomas said.

Fish eggs?

Bleurgh.

'I knew that,' I said. 'I was just mucking about.' I looked around at the mess. The toast had gone everywhere. 'I'll pick it up.'

I peeled a few pieces off the carpet and put them back on to the tray.

'A bit flew into that printer,' Piper said. 'Over on the desk.' She went over and peered into it.

'That's not a printer,' I said. 'It's too big.'

There was a whirring noise.

'Oops,' Piper said. 'I seem to have switched it on.' She stabbed at some buttons. **'Which one's off?'**

We stood there for ages, pressing switches, but it still carried on making a noise. Eventually there was a loud clunk, followed by silence.

Piper grimaced. 'I think we've broken it.'

'What's it doing?' I said.

A hatch rolled up at the front of the machine.

Something popped out.

Eh?

It was a piece of toast, with caviar on.

But it didn't look the same as the bit that had gone in.

It was the same size and shape, but it was white.

Piper reached out and picked it up. 'It's plastic,' she said. 'The machine's turned the toast into plastic.' She stared at me. 'How did that happen?'

Thomas put his hand up. 'I can help you there,' he said. 'It's a **3D** printer. We have one at school. Ours is bigger, but it does the same thing. It produces **3D** copies of whatever you put inside.'

'Really?' I said. 'Of anything?'

Thomas nodded. 'Pretty much. They tried to copy me once, but a teacher came in.'

'Wow.' Piper inspected the plastic toast. 'It's good. You can see all the little fish eggs, and that bit of dill.'

'Excuse me.'

We all jumped.

Viktor stood in the doorway, scowling at us. 'What are you doing?'

Piper hid the piece of plastic toast behind her back. 'I was just admiring your printer,' she said. 'It's very impressive.'

'All museums have them.' Viktor walked over. 'To

repair exhibits. **Would you please step back?** In my experience, children break things merely by looking at them.'

'I haven't touched it, **Steve**,' said Piper. 'I mean, Viktor.'

Grandma bustled in with Rose.

'Poor little doggie,' Grandma said. 'He hates the snow. It took him ages. Did you save me some toast, Ollie?'

'Um … yes.' I passed her the tray.

'You've gone to so much effort, Viktor.' Grandma tucked in. She obviously didn't have a problem with fish eggs. 'Now.' She gulped down the last one. 'Come on, children. We'll have a quick look at the exhibits, and then go and see poor Edna.'

'Ah. Edna. I hope you persuade zem to release her.' Viktor glanced in a mirror and adjusted his beard. 'It vud be a great thing to see her vonce more.'

'You don't have to pretend when it's just us,' Piper said. 'Steve.'

'There vill be tourists downstairs,' Viktor huffed. 'I have to get into ze character.'

'Are you coming? Wonderful.' Grandma must have forgiven him for not being Russian. 'You can tell the children all about the Moscow Star. They do love a good mystery.'

'Von minute.' Viktor walked over to his desk. 'I have a call to make. You go on. I vill join you down there.' He waved us out of the room. 'Remember not to touch the glass.'

We followed Grandma along another vast corridor and down some stairs to the first floor. She pointed to an archway on the right. 'Through here,' she said.

'Woohoo.' Piper bounded ahead. **'Everything's so sparkly!'**

It was. I'm not normally into bling, but the Fabergé stuff was pretty cool.

Each egg had its own cabinet, and a little plaque telling you when it was made, and what was inside.

Thomas pointed at the largest display case. 'Look.

There's a replica of the Moscow Star.'

We went over.

'It's almost as good as the one Piper lost,' Grandma whispered. 'I wonder who made it?'

'Maybe it was Edna?' I said. 'Viktor said she'd done some work for him.'

Thomas looked surprised. 'Wouldn't she have mentioned it?'

'Oh no.' Grandma shook her head. 'Forgers have to be discreet. It's rule number one in *Every Con's Guide to Getting Away With It*. Not, of course, that I have a copy.' She gave a little cough.

Piper was reading the plaque, which gave details of the theft.

'There's a reward!' she said. 'Twenty-five thousand roubles! What's a rouble worth, Ollie?'

I shrugged. 'About a pound?'

Piper gasped. 'Oh my,' she said. 'That's loads. I could probably buy a caravan and the balloon.'

'Um, it's not quite a pound,' Thomas said.

'You can have my share, Piper.' Grandma patted her on the shoulder. 'My reward will be seeing Viktor's face when we return the Moscow Star.'

She'd definitely forgiven him for not being Russian.

'You're not just doing it for Viktor,' I said. 'You're returning a lost artwork to the nation, remember?'

'Of course,' Grandma huffed. 'That's the **worthwhile** bit. Every quest has to have one of those, or you don't get in the newspaper.'

'If we do find the egg,' Thomas said, 'I wouldn't be surprised if we get invited to tea at the **Kremlin**.'

'Really?' Grandma looked thrilled.

'Is that a café?' Piper asked.

'It's where the president lives,' Grandma said. 'It's very grand. I bet they serve excellent cake.'

Blimey. We had to get Edna out of jail, make another egg, have supper at Leo's, swap a fake egg for the real one without anyone noticing, and fit in tea at the Kremlin! Mum was expecting us back by Thursday!

'Let's hope it all goes to plan,' I muttered.

Grandma gave me a pat. 'We have Rose, Ollie. Of course it will.'

'Where is he?' Piper asked. 'I haven't seen him for ages.'

'Just here. Nice and snug under my coat.' Grandma took him out and held him up to the cabinet. 'There you go, Rose. You can get a feel for what we're about to do.'

Rose didn't look particularly interested, but he did lick the glass.

Viktor suddenly appeared behind us.

'Is that saliva?' He sounded horrified. He pulled a cloth out of his pocket. 'I'm going to have to ask you to take your dog out, if you don't mind.'

'It's lucky saliva.' Grandma looked indignant.

'Lucky?' Viktor's eyebrows would have shot into his hair, if he'd had any. **'How can saliva be lucky?'**

'Should we go?' I said. If we started to explain about Rose, we'd be here all day. 'We don't want to miss visiting time.'

'You certainly don't.' Viktor ushered us towards the door. 'Best of luck. And should you manage to secure Edna's release, do let her know she's welcome here.'

'We certainly will.' Grandma beamed. 'You're so kind.'

'Just out of interest, Viktor,' Piper said. 'The Moscow Star?'

Viktor froze. **'What about it?'**

'The night it was stolen, why didn't the alarms go off?'

Viktor blinked. 'The thief got into the basement and cut the power.'

'Oh.' Piper pulled her hat on. 'I guess that could never happen now?'

'Never.' Viktor shook his head. 'Security is much improved. The basement door has been fitted with a combination lock.' He gave a little laugh. 'To switch the electricity off, you'd have to know my birthdate.'

'Clever.' Piper looked admiring. 'And nothing's been stolen since?'

'Not a single thing,' said Viktor.

We walked down the steps of the museum and on to the snowy pavement. Grandma was striding ahead.

'This way,' she called. 'Along the riverbank.'

'Wow,' Piper said. 'Look at all the **skaters**.'

'The ice here gets really thick,' Thomas said. 'You could drive a bus on it.'

I wasn't surprised to hear that. Russia was freezing. For the first time ever, I appreciated Mum's knitting. My head might be itchy but at least my ears wouldn't drop off.

'Grandma?' I raced after her. 'Do we have a plan?'

'We certainly do.' Grandma was looking pleased with herself. 'It just came to me.'

'Just?' I blinked.

Piper had caught up. 'What is it?'

Grandma pulled a newspaper from her bag. 'The

prison need kitchen staff. The advert's here, on the back page. See?' She held it out. 'Viktor circled the address, in case we had to ask for directions. So thoughtful.'

'So we know how to get there?' Piper raised her eyebrows. 'I guess that's the hard part of our mission out of the way.'

'No need to be sarcastic, Piper.' Grandma shoved the paper back in her bag. 'I'm going to apply for the job.'

'Really?' I looked at her in surprise. **'But you can't cook.'**

'How rude.' Grandma looked indignant. 'I'm an excellent cook.'

She isn't.

Thomas sissonned over a pile of snow and galloped alongside me. 'What about us?' he said. 'I thought we were going to help?'

'You can be my assistants,' Grandma said.

'But we're eleven,' I said. 'No one will give us a job.'

'No need to worry. I have everything covered.' Grandma rummaged in her bag and pulled out **three false beards**. 'I borrowed them from Viktor's office.' She handed us one each.

Mine was ginger, with crumbs in it.

'Keep your hats and coats on,' Grandma said. 'They'll bulk you out. The prison's up there. The building backing on to the river. Let me do the talking.'

St Petersburg Reformatory didn't look like the sort of place you'd get anyone out of easily. I wasn't even sure we'd get in, to be honest. The guard on the gate wasn't at all friendly until Grandma showed him the advert. Then he smirked, and waved us through.

'Where now?' asked Piper.

'Reception, I suppose?' Grandma said. 'Follow those arrows.'

The guard must have called ahead, as we were met by a lady with a sticky label on her coat. It had 'Anya' written on it, in red pen.

'Good day.' She held out her hand for Grandma

to shake. 'I am Head of Prison Employment.'

'Oh good. You speak English.' Grandma looked delighted. 'Because that's what we are. English cooks. Well, I am.' She gestured towards us. 'They are my assistants. We go everywhere together. Like a troupe.'

Anya looked us up and down and sniffed. 'Russians all learn English – though the English do not seem to bother with any language other than their own.'

Well, that was a bit rude! I know **loads** of words in Spanish and I'm only in Year Six. I didn't say anything though, as I was in an interview.

Thomas put his hand up. 'Actually,' he said, 'I'm studying Russian. May I try some out?'

Anya shrugged. 'If you must.'

'Я люблю вашу шляпу,' Thomas said. 'Это довольно.'

Anya blinked. She reached up and felt the top of her head, and then looked confused. 'Errm. Thank you,' she said.

'What did you say?' Piper whispered.

Thomas looked embarrassed. 'I thought I said I was happy to be here, but thinking about it, I might have said I liked her hat.'

'She's not wearing a hat,' I said.

'I know,' said Thomas gloomily. 'I told you I was in **catch-up** classes.'

Anya gave her head a little shake, and took out a notepad. She turned to Grandma.

'Have you experience?'

'Oh yes.' Grandma nodded. 'My cooking is renowned.' She clasped her hands. 'I present my own

TV show, *Naked Baking*, in fact.'

Anya nodded and made a note. Then she looked at me.

'You?'

I wasn't sure what to say. I'd never had a job interview before.

I stared at her for a bit and then I said I liked washing up. (Obviously that wasn't true. I wouldn't normally lie, but we needed the job.)

'So do I,' Piper said. What a copycat! Her beard was slipping. Anya didn't seem to notice.

Thomas raised his hand. 'And I,' he said, 'have a level two diploma in scouring, and it would be a pleasure to work with you.'

Then he sneezed.

Anya raised her eyebrows.

She turned to Grandma.

'You may have the job,' she said. Then she pointed at me and Piper. 'And you two, also.'

'Congratulations,' Piper whispered.

'Not you.' Anya pointed at Thomas. 'You have a cold.'

'No, I don't,' protested Thomas. 'I'm just **allergic.**'

'To what?' Anna looked around.

'Um ... nothing,' Thomas said, quickly.

Too late. Anya had spotted Rose, who was draped around Grandma's shoulders. She frowned. 'No dogs in the kitchen,' she said. 'You'll have to take him out.'

'Gracious.' Grandma blinked. 'I would never dream of bringing an animal to work. Especially a dog.'

Anya gave a little cough, and pointed.

'Oh!' Grandma gave a little laugh. 'This is not a dog. This is a stole. Beautiful, isn't it? Used to belong to my dear late mother.' She gave Rose a stroke. 'When I think of the places this has been, the theatres, the—'

Rose yapped.

'No dogs,' Anya said.

Grandma scowled. She unwound Rose from her neck. 'Give me a minute. I'll leave him with the guard.'

It didn't take her long to leave him with the guard,

but Anya didn't seem to notice. She didn't notice Grandma's bulging handbag, either.

'This way,' she said.

Anya marched ahead. Every now and then she'd stop to unlock a set of metal gates, which she ushered us through, and then locked behind us. I started to worry. **Even if we found Edna, how would we get her out?**

Grandma started to embellish her CV.

'I didn't mention the cake,' she said. 'The one I made for the royal wedding. I mean, I was busy, but one always makes time for the queen, doesn't one?'

'Really?' said Anya, speeding up.

Grandma speeded up too. 'You should have seen it. A pyramid of four thousand gold-plated choux buns.'

'Is that so?' Anya didn't seem very impressed, but that didn't stop Grandma.

'There was a slight problem with the turtle doves inside. Someone's mother said they were a health and safety issue.' Grandma gave me a glare.

Eh? She couldn't blame Mum for something she'd made up!

'Here are ze kitchens.' Anya ground to a halt. She unlocked a large metal door and flung it open.

Wow.

The kitchens were **big**.

Anya strode inside. 'There are four hundred prisoners,' she said. 'They are not polite about the food. The last cook stayed two days.'

'Well, I can assure you we are here for the long term,' Grandma lied. 'No need to worry about us letting you down.'

'You must get on,' Anya said. 'Lunch is in an hour.' She handed Grandma a sheet of paper. 'The menu for the week. Please stick to it.'

We peered at the list. There was only one thing on it.

Herring and beetroot soup.

'Now.' Anya flung open an enormous fridge. 'The

herring is in here.'

'They don't smell very fresh,' whispered Piper.

'And over here.' Anya lifted the lid off a crate. 'The beetroot.'

Grandma gave a shudder.

I looked inside. There were hundreds. I hoped we weren't expected to **peel** them.

Anya pointed to a large jar on the side. 'Spices. Do not forget. Use plenty. And there is rye bread also.' She gestured towards a pile of solid-looking loaves. 'You will need to slice them.'

'Food for kings,' approved Grandma. 'You treat your prisoners well.'

'Too well.' Anya sniffed. She turned to Thomas. 'The washing up.' She waved towards two massive sinks stacked high with pans. 'When that is done, you will serve the

143

lunch.' She pointed to a hatch on the far wall. 'Keep it bolted till then.'

'Very good.' Grandma saluted.

'Oh.' Anya had been heading for the door, but she stopped. 'One last thing.' She pulled open a small door built into the wall beside the sink. 'This is the **rubbish chute**.'

'Wonderful,' said Thomas. 'So useful.'

'Indeed,' said Anya. 'It takes the rubbish to a courtyard, to be taken away at the end of each day.'

'Is that so?' Grandma gave me a nudge. I looked at her. **Was she thinking what I was thinking?**

Anya smirked. 'All the prisoners think it would be a wonderful way to escape. Every week we have one sneaking into the rubbish, but the bags are checked before they leave the prison.'

Oh. Maybe not, then.

'If they had this,' Anya waved a **large key**, 'it would be a different story. They could unlock the back gate and stroll away.'

'And the key is kept where?' Grandma looked nonchalant.

'The key is in my pocket, always.' Anya gave a little bow. 'Good luck. I will see you later.'

'**Right.**' **As soon** as the door had closed behind Anya, Grandma let Rose out of her handbag. Thomas sneezed. 'I thought she said he wasn't allowed?' he said.

'I don't think she did,' said Grandma. 'I never heard her say that.'

Piper found us some aprons. 'Have you got a recipe?' she asked, as we tied them on.

'It's **soup**.' Grandma pulled open the fridge. 'How hard can it be?'

I raised my eyebrows. Grandma doesn't do a lot of cooking, but even so, she's still on first-name terms with Great Potton fire service.

I guessed she was right though. It was only soup.

'Give me a hand with this pan, Ollie.' Grandma pointed at a massive one balanced on a rack.

We got it down and pushed it across to the fridge. Then we pulled the herring out into it. I tried not to breathe. Were they **supposed** to smell like that?

'Don't you have to cut the heads off?' Piper asked

'No,' Grandma said. 'They add flavour. I mean, the **eyeballs** might float – but we can skim those off later.'

We hoisted the pan on to the cooker.

Grandma stood on a stool and peered into it. 'Soup needs to be runny, from what I remember,' she said. 'We'll add some water.' She pointed. 'Fill that jug, will you?'

I took it across to one of the sinks. **Oh**. There was no way I could get to the tap without moving stuff. I prodded a pile of bowls. **Bleurgh**. They looked like they'd been there a while.

Luckily, Thomas offered to help. He was very enthusiastic. He cleared everything out in no time and then started looking for washing-up liquid. I looked at his neat piles of crockery. Maybe he wasn't sucking up when he offered to do stuff? **Maybe he**

actually enjoyed it?'

'There you go.' He handed me the full jug.

'Thanks,' I said.

As I carried it back to the cooker, I noticed Rose, over by the door.

What was he chewing on?

I handed the jug to Grandma, and then went over to see.

'Rose?'

He ran off.

Piper helped me corner him by the fridge and I wrestled whatever it was from his jaws.

It was a key.

Piper blinked. 'It's Anya's.'

We looked at each other. It **couldn't** be. She wouldn't have just dropped it. It must be a key for something else. The serving hatch, maybe?

I looked at the tag.

There was something printed on it in Russian that I didn't understand.

Under that, though, were some words in English.
Written in red pen.

KEY TO BACK GATE.

'Grandma!'

'What, dear?' Grandma was
bashing away at the herring
with the end of a rolling
pin. 'This is going to be
delicious. I'm tenderising
it. I saw that naked man do
it on the telly once.'

She saw what I was
holding. 'Gracious.' She
dropped the rolling pin and
climbed down from her
stool. 'Well,' she said. '**What wonderful luck**. I had
absolutely NO idea how we were going to get Edna
out of here.'

'You **said** you had a plan,' Piper said, accusingly.

'I have hundreds of plans,' Grandma said. 'Most of

them are amazing. This one still needed some work.'

She climbed back up. 'We'd better get on with this soup, or there'll be a riot. Is there any more water, Ollie?'

We realised it would take hours to fill the pan with the jug so we found a bit of hosepipe and used that. Then it took us a while to get the cooker to work, because Grandma said it was gas, so we spent ages looking for matches, but it turned out to be electric. Piper turned it on and we left the herring to simmer and went to get the beetroots.

'No need to peel them,' Grandma said. 'We can use them as they are.'

She started lobbing them into the pan. I threw a few too, and then Piper had a go and then we started throwing them at each other and so did Grandma. One of hers flew into the sink and broke a few plates, and Thomas got covered in suds, but he didn't seem to mind.

He did remind us of the time though, so we stopped

throwing beetroot and got on with it.

'I'll cut up the bread,' Piper said. 'Is there a knife?'

Grandma found one in a drawer, and then went back to the soup.

She tipped the spices in with the herring and gave everything a good stir.

My eyes started to water. 'Were you supposed to use the whole jar?' I asked.

'I expect so,' Grandma said. She beamed at us. 'Doesn't it smell wonderful?'

'I **still** think the herring could have been fresher,' Piper said.

Grandma held out the ladle. 'Have a taste, Ollie?'

'Thanks,' I said. 'Maybe later?'

'We need some bowls,' Grandma said. 'Could you get them? Don't worry if they're not clean. No one will notice. Piper, how are you getting on with those loaves?'

Piper put the knife down. 'They won't cut,' she said. 'I think they're fossilised. We'll have to serve them as they are.'

I bet she hadn't tried very hard. 'I'll have a go,' I said.

'Be my guest,' Piper said. She handed me the knife. **Gosh**, they **were** a bit hard.

'I think we should serve them as they are,' I said.

Grandma looked up at the clock. 'Right,' she said. 'Are we all set?'

'What exactly is the plan?' Piper asked. 'You know. The one that still needs work?'

'We'll open the hatch. We'll serve the soup. When Edna comes up we'll smuggle her a note.'

'Have you written one?' I asked.

'I knew I'd forgotten something,' said Grandma. 'Is there any paper?'

We couldn't find any.

'We'll change that bit then,' Grandma said. 'When Edna comes up, you'll have to whisper the message. Tell her to **sneak into the kitchen** as soon as she gets a chance.'

'Then what?' I asked. 'The guards are bound to notice.'

'The minute she's here – you slam the hatch and bolt it.'

'OK,' I said.

'As soon as the serving hatch is bolted, we go headfirst down the rubbish chute. Time will be of the essence, so no hanging about. Then out the gate.' Grandma held up the key. 'And back to the museum.'

'Shall I look after that?' Piper offered. 'I've got pockets.'

'No, Piper,' Grandma said sternly. 'Not after what happened to the egg.'

Piper muttered something under her breath. I got the impression it was rude.

I rattled the hatch. It didn't look like it would keep anyone out for long. 'It sounds simple,' I said, 'but do you think it **will** be?'

Grandma pretended not to hear. She slopped a ladleful of herring soup into a bowl and handed it to me.

I took it. 'You don't think we might get caught?'

'Well, **of course** we might.' Grandma skimmed the top of the soup with the ladle. 'Should I take the eyeballs out, or leave them in?'

I stared at her. If we got locked up, **Mum would be furious.**

Grandma filled another bowl. 'I wouldn't worry, Ollie. A few weeks in a correctional facility never does anyone any harm. Not that I'd know, of course.'

Piper went over to unbolt the hatch. She pushed it up a few centimetres and leant across the counter to peer underneath.

When she turned around, she looked worried. 'There's an **awful lot of guards** out there,' she said. 'I'm not sure Edna will get the chance to "pop through the hatch".'

'We'll distract them,' said Grandma. 'Create a diversion.'

'How?' Thomas asked.

Grandma shrugged. 'I'm sure something will come to me,' she said. 'Pass up some more bowls, would you? We need to make sure there's enough for everyone, before we have ours.'

Have ours? Was she kidding?

Once we'd filled as many bowls as we could find,

Piper rolled the hatch all the way up.

WOW. The dining hall was enormous. I could hardly see the other side.

Long tables stretched across it, and benches ran between them.

Apart from the walls, which were a yellowy concrete colour, everything was grey.

There weren't any windows. The only light came from a fluorescent tube running along the ceiling. It kept flickering.

Piper hadn't been exaggerating. There were loads of guards. Standing all around the walls. And when the hatch went up it seemed like every single one had turned to look in my direction.

I gulped.

They didn't look very nice.

'They can smell my wonderful soup,' Grandma said. 'I expect they're hoping there'll be some left over.'

'There won't be,' said Piper. 'Everyone will want seconds, definitely.' She poked at an eyeball.

'They're coming,' I said.

A set of double doors crashed open and the prisoners started to file through. They seemed very orderly, shuffling towards the hatch in a neat line. None of them looked particularly scary, either, which I was pleased about.

Grandma had put me in charge of handing out the soup. Piper was in charge of the bread. She had the easier job, to be fair, because I kept slopping stuff everywhere, and also, I kept having to mime that, **yes**, it was soup and **yes**, you could eat it.

'Have you seen Edna yet?' Thomas brought some more bowls across.

I peered out the hatch and along the queue. Everyone was wearing grey stripes, and I'd only seen ever Edna with her duffel coat hood up. Even so, she wasn't hard to spot. **'She's there,'** I said.

As she approached, I tried to catch her eye, but I'd forgotten Piper and I were in disguise. She just gave me a strange look.

'Edna,' I hissed, from behind my beard. 'It's us.'

Edna's eyebrows shot into her hair. She checked over her shoulder. Then she leant across the counter. 'About blooming time,' she muttered. 'Can't believe Florence **abandoned** me like that.'

I could see a guard looking so I picked up a bowl and did my soup miming thing.

'What's the score?' Edna muttered. 'File in the loaf? Tow-truck at midnight?'

'**Cooee.**' Grandma waved from the stove. 'Good to see you, Edna.'

'You have to get in here,' I hissed. 'Then it's sorted.'

Edna scratched her chin. 'Difficult,' she said. 'They watch. All the time. Especially that one, with the hat. I'll have to bribe him. Pass over the cash.'

I blinked. 'I haven't got any,' I said.

Edna scowled. 'Your gran said you were in the scouts. Aren't you supposed to be prepared?'

'I haven't done the bribery and corruption badge yet,' I said. 'Hang on. I'll ask Grandma.'

Grandma only had 38p. It wasn't enough.

I went back to Edna. 'Can't you **distract** him?' I said. 'Spill a drink or something? Then hop over while he's mopping it up?'

I'd thought that was a good idea, but Edna stared at me for a long time. Then she leant across the counter. 'This is **prison**,' she hissed. 'Not Great Potton Preschool.'

It wasn't going well. The queue behind Edna were starting to get fidgety and it wasn't just the guard in the hat looking over now.

Piper noticed. **'Move along,'** she bellowed.

I handed Edna her bowl. 'Just try,' I said. 'We can't get you out otherwise.'

Edna wasn't listening. She was looking into the bowl with horror.

'There's plenty for seconds,' Grandma called from the stove.

Edna stalked off, muttering.

'Don't worry, Ollie.' Piper handed out a loaf. 'Lunch isn't over yet. I'm sure she'll think of something.'

I **looked out** across the dining hall. We'd done a pretty good job in getting the soup out, and a few of the prisoners were even eating it – though most had pushed it aside and were glaring at our serving hatch.

I felt a bit nervous. I hoped they weren't going to make a fuss.

Edna was sitting at the end of a table with her back to us. I wondered if she'd make a break for it. She could be over here in a couple of seconds and we could slam down the hatch an— What was she doing?

OMG! She was going with my plan! She'd knocked her drink over.

'Ready Piper,' I said. 'She's coming.'

Piper stopped wiping the side and looked up.

'Eh?' she said. 'No, she's not.'

Oh. Edna had been right. It wasn't like preschool. No one had rushed over to mop anything up and she was still sitting there.

'How's it going?' Grandma had got down from her stool and was eating a biscuit. 'I'd have had some of the soup,' she said, 'if it wasn't for the beetroot. Vegetables **do** ruin things.'

I rather fancied a biscuit myself and was just about to ask Grandma for one when a commotion broke out at the back of the hall.

'What's going on?' Piper tried to see.

Thomas scrambled up on to the counter for a better look. 'I think a prisoner's been taken ill.' He craned his neck. 'Oh. More than one, actually.'

I scanned the room. The inmates were starting to mutter amongst themselves. They all looked a bit pale.

Green, in fact.

The muttering got louder. Then someone shouted,

'Ze poison.'

Three people fell
face first into their
bowls.

'Gracious,'
said Grandma.
'Look at them.
Dropping like
flies. There must
be a bug going
round.'

'Do you think it was the
soup?' I said.

Grandma looked outraged. 'Of course not,' she
said. 'How could it be the soup? I did **exactly** what
Anya said. Fish, beetroot and spices. It was delicious.
Everyone said so.'

I wasn't sure they had.

'I knew the herring wasn't fresh,' Piper said. 'I bet
it was that.'

I picked up the empty spice jar and looked at it. The original label had been crossed out and someone had written 'Spices' underneath, in red pen.

That was weird.

Anya's name badge had been written in red pen.

And the writing on the key.

I didn't have time to think about it. The place was in uproar. The guards were racing up and down the rows, pulling people out of their bowls and radioing for help.

Edna got up from her bench and sauntered over. 'Is this a good time?' she said. 'Looks like they enjoyed your soup, Florence. Top idea.'

Grandma glared at her. 'It was **NOT** the soup,' she said. 'I'm an excellent cook.'

'I'd hurry up, if I were you,' Piper said to Edna. 'Before someone notices you're here.'

I thought Edna hopped over the counter quite nimbly, for somebody so stout.

Piper **slammed** the hatch down.

'Quick,' I shouted. I pushed one bolt across and Piper did the other.

'Do you think anyone saw?' she asked.

'No time to find out. We're going down the chute.' Grandma shoved Edna towards it. 'This way.'

Someone started to bang on the hatch. Those bolts wouldn't hold for long. We had to hurry.

Grandma flung open the door in the wall and Edna dived in headfirst.

'Now you, Ollie,' Grandma ordered. 'Then Piper and Thomas. I'll keep the hordes at bay.' She waved a spatula.

I decided to go feet first.

Oh. I climbed back out.

'What's wrong?' Piper asked.

'Edna's stuck.'

I could see her feet and hear some muffled shouts. There was no way past. It looked like she'd got wedged in a bend.

'I'll sort it,' Grandma said. 'Mind out of the way.'

She reached in and jabbed Edna a couple of times with the spatula, but it didn't make any difference. Edna was well and truly jammed.

There was another thump on the hatch. I looked round in a panic. If they started throwing those loaves, we wouldn't stand a chance.

'The cooking oil!' I pointed. 'Piper. **Quick**.'

Piper grabbed it from the counter and handed it to me. I wrenched the cap off and started to pour.

'Give her another push, Grandma.'

Grandma leant in with the spatula for one last swipe.

Yay! It had worked. Edna shot off down the pipe.

I didn't waste any time. The hatch was giving way. 'Hurry, Piper,' I shouted, as I shot after Edna.

The rubbish chute was just like the slide at Great Potton Pool, though it smelt worse. (Not that much worse, actually.) Luckily, the oil speeded everything up so it wasn't long before I flew out into fresh air.

I landed on Edna, who was half buried in fish heads and peelings.

'Watch it.' She pushed me off and struggled to her feet. Then Piper shot out. Her feet hit Edna squarely in the back.

I didn't hear what Edna said, as she was face down in herring heads again, but I'm pretty sure it was rude.

Thomas landed on both of them.

'Oh, I'm terribly sorry,' he said. He helped Piper up, and then they both pulled Edna out. 'Where are we?'

'In a skip, by the looks of it,' I said.

I stood on a pile of turnips and peered over the edge. I could see the gate. It was on the far side of the courtyard, embedded in a high stone wall. It really was the only way out. I squinted up the chute.

Where was Grandma? She should be here by now.

'What's she doing?' Edna spat out a gill. 'They'll be after us in a minute.'

'She was looking for the key,' Piper said. 'She insisted I had it, but I didn't.'

'I'm here!' Grandma shot out with Rose.

Edna went flying again.

We helped her up and brushed her down, but she didn't seem very grateful. There was a lot of muttering. This time it was definitely rude.

'Hurry.' Grandma handed Rose to Piper and

climbed over the edge of the skip. 'They'll be on to us any minute.'

We scrambled after her.

'Your beard's wonky, Ollie,' Thomas said.

I adjusted it. 'You do have the key, don't you, Grandma?'

Grandma held it up. 'It was in my pocket all along,' she said. 'I was sure I'd given it to Piper.'

'No need to apologise,' Piper huffed.

'I thought the prisoners had broken through the hatch,' I said.

'If they had, Ollie,' Grandma said, 'it would have been because they wanted the recipe for the soup. I expect it was the best thing they'd ever tasted.'

'Great idea to put something in it.' Edna grunted in approval. 'Clever. What was it? Arsenic? Cyanide?'

Grandma scowled. 'As I said, Ed—'

'I can hear shouting,' Piper said. **'Can we get a move on?'**

'Good idea.' Grandma charged towards the gate.

168

'Come on.'

I kept glancing over my shoulder but no one came down the chute.

'Here we go.' Grandma brandished the key, then pushed it into the lock.

I held my breath. Please let it open. I didn't want to think about what would happen if it didn't. We could be locked up for years. I'd probably have to share a cell with Thomas, who'd be doing his pliés all over the place. I'd have to eat herring. Mum and Dad woul—

There was a click, and the gate swung outwards.

'Yay!' Piper gave a little skip. **'We're free!'**

'Wonderful,' Grandma said. 'After you, Edna.'

Edna stuck her head round and looked up and down the street outside. 'No one's about,' she said. 'Look casual, though, just in case.'

I untangled some peelings from my fringe and took off my beard.

Grandma handed her apron to Edna. 'Put it on,'

she said. 'You won't stand out as much.'

'Ta.' Edna popped it over her head. 'Does it suit me?'

I looked at her. The apron said *Property of St Petersburg Reformatory* on the front.

'Oh yes,' I said. 'It's very you.'

22

It's quite hard to look nonchalant when you're covered in herring. And I couldn't help checking over my shoulder every five seconds. No one seemed to be following us. **Yet.**

We took a back route, and went into the museum through a side door. Grandma led the way. 'Stay behind us for now, Edna,' she ordered. 'There'll be tourists about.'

'Ah. You're back.' Viktor popped out from behind a suit of armour. Blimey. Anyone would think he'd been lying in wait. He had a tin of polish in one hand and a duster in the other, and looked strangely delighted to see us.

'I heard there was a disturbance at the prison? I do hope you didn't get caught up in—' His face convulsed with horror. **'What's that smell?'**

'My perfume?' Grandma said. 'Do you like it?

Viktor held the duster to his nose.

'Charming,' he muttered. 'Wonderful fishy overtones.'

His eyes were watering.

Maybe we should shower?

'And Edna?' Viktor lowered the duster and looked around eagerly. 'Did you manage to see her?'

'We certainly did.' Grandma beamed. 'It was as I thought. A misunderstanding. The politysia were so apologetic.' She stepped back. 'Here she is.'

'Edna.' Victor flung open his arms. 'How wonderful to see you.'

'Viktor?' Edna looked astonished. 'Blimey. Thought you'd have retired.'

'Soon, Edna. **Very** soon.' Viktor's teeth glinted. 'We must catch up. Would you care to join me in my office for a teacake?' He offered her his arm.

Edna took it. 'Fabby,' she said. 'I love teacakes.'

Viktor started to steer her down the corridor.

'Wait for us.' Grandma trotted along behind.

'Oh.' Viktor looked surprised. 'Should you not go and freshen up?

Grandma blinked. 'Well. We would – but we travelled light. We don't have anything to change into.'

'Ah.' Viktor stopped. 'I can help with that.' He pointed back down the corridor. 'We have a room of costumes for school visits. You'll find something there.'

'How kind.' Grandma glared at him.

Viktor turned back to Edna. 'Come,' he said. 'You must tell me what you've been up to since we last met.'

They trotted off down the corridor.

I stared after them. **How come Edna got to go off and have teacakes?** She was covered in herring too.

Grandma clearly felt the same. She huffed and puffed all the way to the costume room, and when we got there she clattered around in the racks and threw things all over the place.

Thomas patted her arm. 'I'm sure Viktor didn't mean to be rude,' he said. 'Edna's an old friend. I expect he'll save you a teacake.'

'I should hope so,' Grandma muttered, 'bearing in mind what we're here for.' She pulled out a dress and held it up. 'What do you think?

It was pink, and shiny, and had an enormous skirt that stuck out all round.

'That's lovely,' Thomas said, admiringly.

'Isn't it?' Grandma pulled it on. 'Edna will be sorry she didn't come with us. I'm going to look absolutely **delightful** in this.'

'It's a ball gown.' Piper had found a fetching bonnet for Rose, and was tying it under his chin. 'Are you going to one?'

'I might.' Grandma admired herself in a mirror. 'If there is one, I'm sure I'll be invited to it.'

I rummaged through heaps of stuff, but I couldn't find anything that wasn't frilly, or embroidered, or trimmed with fur.

'How about these?' Piper said. She held up some velvet pantaloons.

'Ha, funny,' I said.

'Look, there's a shirt – and a waistcoat to match.'

The shirt had ruffles all over it, and billowing sleeves.

'Oh.' Thomas looked thrilled. 'That's **lovely**. May I wear it, Ollie, if you don't want to?'

'Be my guest.' I carried on looking.

In the end, Grandma told me off for taking too long.

I ended up in pantaloons and a shirt, like Thomas.

'Wow.' Piper giggled. 'Cool.'

I glowered at her. She didn't look particularly fashionable in her big skirt and flowery blouse, either.

'Right.' Grandma popped a sparkly clip in her hair. 'Let's go.'

'How long have we got? Piper asked.

'Leo's sending a car for us at seven. **That gives Edna four hours to make another egg**. Loads of time.'

It didn't seem like loads to me.

We found Edna with Viktor, in his office. They were laughing together, and toasting teacakes.

Edna still had her stripy jumpsuit on, though it was mainly covered up with the apron and a beige mac, which gaped around the middle. For a minute I thought she'd found some earrings from somewhere, but then I realised they were beetroot peelings.

'We need to get rid of Viktor,' Grandma whispered. 'So we can talk freely.'

'Leave it to me.' Piper walked over. 'Viktor?'

He turned. 'What?'

'There's a child with a **lollipop**,' Piper said. 'In the egg room. I'm sure his parents are supervising, but you said—'

I'd never seen anyone move so fast. Viktor was gone.

The minute the door slammed behind him, Grandma raced over.

'Edna,' she said, 'you have to make us **another** egg.'

Edna looked at her. 'I only just made you one,' she said. 'What happened to it?'

'Piper lost it,' Grandma said.

'Hey!' said Piper.

Edna shrugged. 'Sorry,' she said. 'Can't.'

'Why?' Grandma said. 'We brought all the stuff.' She held up a packet of gems.

'I'm busy.' Edna leant back in her chair.

'No, you're not,' Grandma said. 'You're having a teacake.'

'I've been offered a job.' Edna took a big bite. 'Starts this evening. Can't let them down. It wouldn't be professional.'

Grandma blinked. 'I got you out of jail! **Twice**.'

Edna shrugged. 'Sorry.' She got to her feet. 'I've committed. Cheerio.' She grabbed another teacake and stomped out.

Grandma stared after her. **'Can you believe that?'** She flung herself into a chair. 'We've come all this way for **nothing**.'

'Hey.' Piper wasn't listening. She was staring over at Viktor's desk. 'Tell you what. How about I make it?'

'Make what?' I said.

'The Moscow Star!'

We all stared at her.

'Piper,' I said, as kindly as I could. 'When you made that nativity scene last year, Little Baby Jesus was mistaken for a chipolata.'

'That wasn't my fault. I left him till last and the bell rang for break.'

'But a Fabergé egg?' I said. 'That's much harder than Jesus.'

'Not if I use the **3D** copier,' Piper said.

Grandma sprang to her feet. 'That's a fabulous idea, Piper. In fact, I was just about to suggest it myself.'

'You'll have to get rid of Viktor for an hour,' Piper said. 'The museum shuts soon. I'll borrow the replica from downstairs. I'll copy it, then put it back.'

'What about the alarm?' Thomas said.

'The code to the basement door is Viktor's date of birth.' She picked up the photo from the desk and pointed at the date on the back. 'He was seven when this was taken – so we subtract seven years.' She jotted down a number. 'Here you go.' She handed it to me.

'Eh?' I looked at her.

'The basement. It's where the fuse box is. You go and turn the electricity off, and I'll get the egg.'

'OK,' I said. 'Grandma, you'll have to keep Viktor out of the way.'

Grandma shoved Rose into my arms. 'Take him for luck. I'll ask Viktor to show me some sights. I'll keep him out as long as I can.'

We watched from the office window.

'There they go,' I said.

'Edna's with them,' Piper said. 'I bet your gran's not pleased about that.'

The three of them walked down the museum steps to the street. Viktor was swathed in his furs and he'd lent some to Edna. As she was quite short, they dragged behind her, like a train. Grandma kept stepping on it. **On purpose**, I think.

'Are you ready?' Piper asked

I was, but Rose had started to look like he needed to go and do his business.

Thomas offered to take him out, which was good, as I didn't want to miss any of the fun.

'Thanks,' I said. 'Come on, Piper.'

Thomas sneezed. 'Has he got a lead?' he

called after us.

'Somewhere,' I said. 'Don't worry. He doesn't **usually** run off.'

We raced along the corridor and down the stairs to the egg room. Piper pointed at a light flashing in the corner. 'That's the alarm. When you cut the current, it'll go off. Give me ten seconds. That should be enough.'

'OK.' I headed for the door.

'Have you got the code?' Piper called after me.

'Yep.' I waved the bit of paper at her.

'Ollie.'

I stopped. 'What?'

'Don't go and get locked in, will you?' she said. 'Because that's the sort of thing you do, and I won't have time to come and get you out.'

It took me a while to find the basement. Piper had said the door was next to the kitchen – but so was a coat cupboard and what turned out to be the ladies' toilets.

I carefully typed Viktor's birthdate into the keypad.

The door clicked open.

I peered down a flight of rickety wooden steps. It was ever so dark down there. I felt around for a light switch – but there didn't seem to be

one. I should have brought a torch. Never mind. I'd just have to prop the door open.

I looked around for something to use. Most of the stuff in the hall looked fairly priceless, so in the end I took off my shoe and used that.

Even so, it was still dark. I heard a rustle as I felt my way down, and tried not to think about rats. **There must be a light switch somewhere!**

I groped around the wall at the bottom ...

Finally!

A bulb came on overhead. It wasn't very bright, and kept flickering as if it was about to go out – but at least I could see that I was in a passageway, with a door at the end. Next to it, up on the wall, was the fuse box.

It was quite high up. I'd need something to stand on, but there was nothing in the passage. Maybe there was something on the other side of that door? I tried the handle, and it wasn't locked so I opened it and stuck my head round.

It was some kind of workshop. The walls were bare brick, and there weren't any windows. Tools were lined up along a bench, and at the end of it was a lamp.

The lamp was on.

That was weird. I looked around nervously. There didn't seem to be anyone down here. It must have been left on by mistake.

There was a stool under the bench. That'd do. I carried it into the passage and stood on it. Right. I flipped down the front of the fuse box and looked along the switches. There wasn't anything helpful written under them in red pen, like there was at the prison, so I couldn't work out which switch was which. I'd have to use the main one, and that would turn everything off – including the lights down here. I didn't like the idea of that, but it couldn't be helped.

I reached up and flipped it. I shut my eyes at the same time, so I couldn't see I was all alone down here, in the dark, with the rats.

I tried not to count really, really quickly, but when I got to ten, I was worried that I hadn't given Piper long enough to get the egg, so I counted another five.

I shoved the switch back up.

I opened my eyes. Phew. Light.

I closed the front of the box and got down, and then I went and put the stool back. I didn't feel so nervous now. There was definitely no one down here. I looked along the row of tools. I wondered if Piper would need anything for her egg. Those tweezers, maybe?

I examined a pair, and then pulled open a drawer, which was empty, so then I tried the other.

Eh?

That was weird.

The drawer was stuffed with teacakes.

I blinked. **What a funny place to keep teacakes.**

Still. Viktor was a bit nuts.

I pushed the drawer shut.

Then, I heard a distant slam.

I hoped it wasn't the basement door.

I ran out into the passage. Piper would be really cross if I'd locked myself in. She'd specifically told me not to.

I'd just got to the foot of the stairs when the bulb overhead gave a final flicker and went out.

BUM. It was pitch black. The door at the top was definitely shut. I took a deep breath. I was eleven. I was **NOT** scared of the dark.

I made my way up the stairs and felt around for a handle. There wasn't one.

I gave the door a kick and wondered how long it would be before Piper came to find me.

She might not come until she'd finished making the egg.

I sat on the step to wait. I could always go and get a teacake if she took ages.

OMG! I jumped up. Something brushed past my ankle! Was that a rat? That was definitely a rat.

The rat yapped.

Eh? Rats didn't yap.

It wasn't a rat.

It was Rose.

I'd just grabbed him when the door flew open and hit me square in the back.

'OW.'

'Oh, I say, Ollie. Sorry.'

It was Thomas.

'Rose ran off,' he said. 'I saw him scamper in here and then the door slammed. I had to go and get the code from Piper. She got the egg. She's just copying it.'

I wrestled my shoe from Rose's mouth. 'Come on then,' I said. 'I can't wait to see it.'

'What do you think?' Piper held up a white plastic egg.

'Wow.' I went over and had a look, close up. 'That's **incredible**.'

'It is, isn't it?' she said. 'The copier is amazing. It's captured every detail. I just need to paint it.'

'Florence will be thrilled,' Thomas said. 'Well done, Piper.'

'Thanks,' she said. 'Can you go and put the real one back?' She took it out of the copier and handed it to me. 'Viktor would go crazy if he thought it had vanished. It would ruin your gran's surprise.'

'What about the alarm?' I said.

'I reprogrammed it,' she said. 'You'll be fine for the next ten minutes.' She prised the lid off a tin of blue paint. 'Take Rose with you. I don't want any dog hairs in this.'

'OK.' I picked Rose up. 'Come on, Thomas. We'd better hurry.'

'Isn't this fun,' Thomas said, as we raced back down to the egg room.

He slid open the cabinet and I dropped the egg on to the stand. Phew. I closed my eyes in relief. We'd done it.

'Excuse me?'

My eyes flew open.

Oh dear. Viktor
was back. That
was quick. He was
standing in the
doorway, quivering.

He pointed
at Rose. **'Why is
he here?'**

'Sorry, Viktor.' I
picked Rose up and we
started to sidle out past him.

'We just wanted a last look at the eggs. I expect we'll be off in the morning, now we've rescued Edna.'

Viktor looked pleased when I said that, but then he went on for ages about dog hair, and went to get a hoover. Which was lucky, because if he'd gone straight to his office he'd have caught Piper painting the egg.

'Come on.' I dragged Thomas towards the stairs.

'I was going to help,' Thomas said. 'I'm good at hoovering.'

I looked at him. 'You know that stuff you said in the balloon,' I said, 'about doing things so people like you?'

'Yes?' Thomas said. He held on to the banister and did a little plié.

'You don't have to, you know,' I said. 'People are supposed to like you for you.'

Thomas looked confused. 'But I enjoy hoovering,' he said. 'So that's win-win, isn't it?'

'That's not the point,' I said. 'You make the rest of us look bad.'

'Do I?' Thomas blinked.

'Yes. You do. Can't you be ... I don't know. Less good?'

Thomas looked at me. 'OK,' he said. 'I'll have a go.'

'Great,' I said.

Grandma was back too. She didn't look very happy.

'You weren't out for long,' I said.

'Edna said she had stuff to do,' Grandma muttered. 'So we had to come back.'

'I've copied the egg,' Piper said. 'Do you want to see?'

'In a minute.' Grandma stomped over to hang her coat up. **'Oops.'** She knocked one of Viktor's hats off the rack and stepped on it. 'Just look at that,' she said. 'Ruined. What a shame.'

'What's wrong?' I asked.

Grandma booted the flattened hat across the room. **'Nothing,'** she huffed.

'Are you sure?' Thomas said. 'You seem a little out of sorts.'

'Oh. OK then. **It's Viktor**.' Grandma flung herself into a chair. 'He was as nice as pie when we got here – and now Edna's turned up, he keeps asking when we're going home! He's **SO** rude. I've a good mind to abandon the plan.'

'Hey.' Piper looked up from the egg. 'I've spent ages making this!'

'It's been thirty years,' I said. 'They're just catching up.'

'That's as may be. You should have seen them, laughing and walking ahead. They were deliberately leaving me out.'

'Sometimes Thea Harris does that to me,' said Piper. 'It's not very nice.'

'**Everyone** does it to me,' said Thomas, mournfully.

'It's mean,' Grandma huffed. 'I think we should forget the whole thing and go home.'

'No, Grandma. You're doing this for the nation,' I

reminded her. 'Not Viktor. Think of the glory.'

'And the reward,' Piper said. 'Don't forget I'm buying your balloon.'

'It would be a shame not to have tea at the Kremlin,' Thomas said.

Grandma perked up. 'I suppose you're right. I'm not so bothered about the glory, but if there's cake ... let me see the egg, Piper.'

Piper held it up.

Oh.

'That's ... um ... great,' I said.

'It's very good,' Thomas said politely. 'Leo won't be able to tell the difference, I'm sure.'

'It's better from this side.' Piper turned it round. 'I ran out of stars.'

'It's wonderful, Piper.'
Grandma admired it. Then
she looked at her watch.
'We've got an hour. Do you
think it'll be finished by then?'

Piper looked indignant. '**It is** finished,' she said. She started to look through the mess on Viktor's desk. 'I need something to put it in,' she said. 'To protect it.'

I went over to help. I rummaged through a couple of drawers and found a humbug tin that was about the right size. It still had sweets in so I emptied them into Grandma's bag. She liked mints and I was pretty sure Viktor wouldn't miss them.

'Thanks.' Piper took the tin and dropped her egg inside.

'Don't go and lose this one,' Grandma said.

Piper glared at her. 'Who would do something so stupid?' she said.

'Would anyone mind if I tidied a bit?' Thomas skipped across and started to neaten up Viktor's piles of paper. Then he stopped. He picked up a frame and looked closely at at the picture in it. 'Isn't that Anya?' he said.

'Anya? Where?' I peered over his shoulder.

'There.' Thomas pointed. 'The woman beside Viktor.'

The photo must have been taken a while ago, as Viktor had hair. But Thomas was right. **The woman did look like Anya.**

'He said he knew someone at the prison.' Piper said.

'But Anya?' I started to panic. 'Suppose she tells Viktor that Edna escaped? And that we helped her?'

'We were in disguise, Ollie.' Piper turned the photo over. 'It isn't Anya, anyway. It's someone called Tracy. You're such a worrier.'

26

As we sneaked out past the egg room, we could hear the clank of a mop bucket. Viktor certainly liked to keep things clean. There was no sign of Edna. I wondered where she'd gone.

We let ourselves out of the main entrance and down the steps.

'Is everyone clear on the plan?' Grandma hissed.

'Um. Not really,' Thomas said. 'Perhaps you could run through it?'

'We introduce ourselves to Leo as his English relatives. After supper, we'll **persuade** him to show us the egg. I'll **distract** him and Ollie can make the **switch**. Remember to place Piper's dodgy side down. Then we leave in triumph.' Grandma looked pleased with herself. 'Simple.'

'How come I have to do the **risky** bit?' I said.

'I'll do it, if you don't want to,' Thomas offered.

'Well done, Thomas.' Grandma gave him a slap on the back.

Hey!

'I didn't say I wouldn't do it,' I said. 'And Thomas, you said you'd stop doing things for people, remember?'

Thomas looked puzzled. 'But you also said be less good, and stealing a priceless egg is definitely quite less good, isn't it?'

'Yes, bu—'

'For the last time,' said Grandma, 'we are exchanging. **Not stealing**.' She rapped on the window of a large black car that was parked under a street light. **'Cooee,'** she shouted. **'We're here.'**

A man in a hat jumped out of the driver's door and raced round to the pavement. My, his beard was big. He pulled open the passenger door and saluted.

'Thank you ...' Grandma peered at his badge. 'Karl.'

She picked up her skirts and stepped inside. The

rest of us squashed in next to her.

Karl got back behind the wheel and shut the door. He slid back the little glass partition between us and him.

'Eet is not far,' he said. 'Belts on, please.' He shut the partition again.

Grandma looked at Piper. 'Do we have the egg?' she asked.

'It's in the tin, in my pocket,' Piper said. 'I wouldn't **dream** of putting it safely in a plastic box, like I did last time.'

'Good to hear, Piper.' Grandma patted her arm.

As Karl drove us out of the centre, and away from the main roads, I noticed how snowy Russia was. In some places the drifts towered above the car. I hoped we'd be getting a lift back. My pantaloons were **definitely** not suitable for walking in this sort of weather.

We'd only been in the car five minutes when it stopped outside some gates.

They were ever so big, and had spikes along the top.

'We must be here.' Grandma gave Rose a squeeze of excitement. 'Ready, everyone?'

'There's guards.' Piper sounded a bit nervous.

Karl wound his window down, and shouted something over.

'What did he say?' I asked.

'Open the gate?' suggested Thomas.

I stared at him. 'Do you actually know any Russian?' I asked.

'It's a very difficult language,' Thomas said, sulkily.

He was right though.

The gates were opening.

There was no turning back.

Leo's driveway went on for miles. There wasn't much to see. Just banks of snow, and the occasional tree.

'Blimey,' Piper said as we rounded a corner. 'Is that his house? Look at the fountain.'

'It's very fine,' said Thomas. 'The gilding on the roof is to die for.'

I blinked. **Wow**. You didn't see houses like that in Great Potton, even in the posh bits. **It was like a castle!** The front door was wide enough to drive a bus through, and huge pillars rose up either side. On top of each was a curly sculpture, crested with snow.

'Each hand-carved from marble to represent a cheesy snack,' Grandma said, admiringly. 'I read that on Google.'

The car glided to a halt outside the entrance.

'Wow.' Piper pointed. 'Snowmobiles! Perhaps we could ask for a go?'

Grandma didn't wait for Karl. She handed me Rose and hauled herself out. 'This way.' She set off down the path.

'Grandma.' I caught up. 'Suppose we got it wrong? Suppose he doesn't have the egg?'

'Of course he does,' Grandma said. 'Leo stole that egg and we are going to get it back.' She screeched to a halt in front of the mammoth doors. 'Right. We're here.' She reached up and tugged on the bell pull.

We didn't have to wait.

The door swung open.

And there in front of us, in his gigantic hallway, stood **Leo Bolonski**.

27

Blimey.

He wasn't what I expected the king of cheesy snacks to look like, I must say.

He was **tiny**. And **old**. With a lot of **bushy white hair**. Some was on his head, but the rest seemed to sprout from his nose and ears – and of course his chin. He must have been growing that beard since his teens.

He had a great tartan scarf wrapped several times around his neck, and baggy corduroy trousers.

His cardigan looked like something my mum had knitted. His glasses, which were perched on his miniature nose, were the thickest I'd ever seen.

He looked more like a librarian than a billionaire jewel thief.

He held his arms out.

'Florence,' he said. 'My dearest cousin. I am overjoyed you are here. I was so fond of your mother. And you have brought a darling leetle dog.' He reached out to pet Rose, who immediately snapped at him.

'Leo.' Grandma gave a curtsy. 'It was so kind of you to invite us.' She shoved me forward. 'This is Ollie. He's related to me – so that means, of course, he is also related to you.'

'Welcome.' Leo offered me his tiny hand.

I shook it. 'Pleased to meet you,' I said.

Piper shook his hand too, and then Thomas gave a little bow and tried out his Russian again. 'Мы являемся пения труппа,' he said.

Leo's bushy eyebrows shot up. He blinked several

times. 'That is vonderful,' he said. 'I love ze music. I shall look forward greatly. Come. Zis way.'

'What did you say?' I whispered, as we followed Leo down the hall.

'I thought I said I liked his house,' Thomas said.

'I'm not sure you did,' said Piper.

Leo took a sharp right into a large drawing room. 'I have prepared a special Russian tea for my English relations.' He gestured to a laden table. 'Plenty of herring. Ze herring is my **favourite**. Do eat.'

'Lovely,' said Piper weakly.

'Ooh,' Thomas said. 'Delicious.' He tucked in with gusto.

I didn't want to seem rude. I lifted the lid on a large tureen.

'What is it?' asked Piper.

'Cabbage,' I said. 'Boiled, I think.'

There were lots of gherkins, and some hard-boiled eggs, and beetroot cut into fancy shapes. I took a square of toast with fish eggs on. At least I knew what it was. I'd nibble round the edge and give the rest to Rose.

'Ollie!' Piper's mouth fell open. **'Look at the mantelpiece!'**

I looked. **OMG**. There it was. In a little glass case, sparkling in the candlelight.

The Moscow Star.

I couldn't believe Leo had it on display.

'A double bluff,' Thomas whispered.

Grandma had spotted it too. She was so excited she almost choked on a gherkin.

Leo trotted over. "Ow are you finding the food?'

'Fabulous,' said Thomas. 'It's all fabulous.'

'You have a **brilliant** house,' Piper said. 'It's massive.'

Leo nodded. 'Eet is too big for one person,' he said. 'I cannot even see its splendour any more. I am planning on selling and giving ze money to charity.'

'Really?' I said. Given his history of jewel theft, I found that surprising.

'Yes.' Leo nodded. 'I fought hard to become king of the cheesy snack world. Too hard. And for what?' He sighed. 'I have not always done things I am proud of. I wish to make amends. One must try and give back when one can, do you not agree, Florence?'

'Oh, absolutely,' Grandma said. 'It's all about the "giving back", isn't it, children?' She gave me a nudge. 'Did you hear that?' she whispered. 'He's practically giving us permission to take the egg,' she hissed.

I wasn't sure he was.

Thomas put his hand up. 'Mr Bolonski, I hope you don't mind me changing the subject, but is that a Fabergé on the mantelpiece?'

Leo looked a little uncomfortable. 'No, no,' he said. 'Eet is a replica. The Moscow Star. The real one was stolen many years ago.'

'Such a liar,' Grandma muttered in my ear.

Thomas had walked over to the glass case. 'I'm a **massive** fan. I don't suppose I could have a **proper** look?'

Leo seemed reluctant. 'I cannot. It may not be real, but it is still very precious.'

Was that a bead of sweat on his brow?

'Oh, go on,' Grandma said. 'We're family.' She gave him a charming smile.

Leo looked like he was wavering. 'I tell you vot,' he said. 'I will open the case – if first, ze children sing for me.'

'**Sing?**' Grandma exclaimed. 'Of course they will. They are all excellent singers.' She clapped her hands. 'Come on, children. Line up.'

I looked at her in horror. 'I can't sing,' I said.

'Nor can I,' said Piper. 'Sorry.'

'Or me.' Thomas looked apologetic.

Leo frowned. 'But ze boy –' he pointed at Thomas '– ven you came in, said that you ver a singing troupe.'

'Honestly, Thomas.' Piper looked cross. 'You really must stop speaking Russian. It's all right when it's just about you, but now you're getting us involved.'

'Sorry.' Thomas hung his head.

Leo looked mutinous. 'No song, no egg.' He folded his arms and looked stubborn.

'How about a dance?' Piper suggested. 'Thomas can dance. Would that do?'

Leo shrugged. 'It is not as good as ze singing.'

'But Thomas is **very** talented,' Piper said.

'Am I?' Thomas said, nervously.

I frowned at him. **'Yes, you are,'** I said. I gave him a push.

'OK.' Thomas still looked unsure, but he walked into the middle of the room.

Leo pulled a little remote out of his pocket. 'OK, ve shall see. Vot music would you like?'

'You choose,' Thomas said.

Leo pressed play.

It sounded like someone had stepped on a cat.

Rose didn't like it. He yelped at the very first note and shot under the table. Thomas flung his arms into the air. Then he stood there for a bit, motionless, and with his eyes shut.

'What's he doing?' muttered Piper.

The music changed key. Rose whimpered.

Thomas threw himself on to the floor and started to writhe.

My mouth dropped open. What was wrong with him? **Had he been poisoned?**

I glanced nervously at Grandma. She didn't seem worried. She was nibbling on a biscuit.

Thomas wriggled across the floor, like a caterpillar, then **sprang** to his feet. He dashed to a corner and crouched there, flapping his arms, then he did a forward roll and rose up on his knees. His eyes were still closed, and he swayed from side to side with a look of terrible woe on his face.

His final run ended up face down on the floor, where he lay, spreadeagled, until the music finished.

Well.

Piper and I were **dumbstruck.**

Leo liked it.

I've never seen anyone clap so hard.

Thomas got to his feet and gave a little bow.

'Bravo,' Leo shouted. 'Bravo.'

He dashed over and grabbed Thomas by the shoulders. 'You have **such** talent,' he snuffled. 'I am moved.'

'What was that?' I muttered to Grandma.

'Dreadful,' she said. She took another bite of biscuit.

'Um ... well done, Thomas,' said Piper.

'Did you like it?' Thomas came over, beaming. 'It's interpretive dance.'

This was definitely one of those occasions where it was OK to lie.

'Absolutely brilliant,' I said.

'It was **vonderful**.' Leo dabbed his eye with an expensive-looking hanky. 'And now, I vill keep my promise. I vill let you hold ze Moscow Star.'

'The *fake* Moscow Star,' Piper corrected him.

'Ah yes,' Leo said. 'Zat is vot I meant.'

He unlocked the case with a shaking hand. 'Here.' He held the egg aloft for a moment, and then placed it into Thomas's outstretched hands. 'Please be careful. Eet may only be a copy, but I am very fond of it.'

Wow. Thomas's face. He was agog. He was holding the Moscow Star. **The real thing.**

It was **glorious**.

STUNNING.
AMAZING.

And apart from the size and the colour it didn't look anything like the one Piper had made.

Which was worrying.

'Leo,' Grandma called more loudly than she needed to, from the far side of the room. 'Could you tell me a little more?' She gestured to a painting. 'The subject looks familiar. Is it a relative of ours?'

'Ah.' Leo turned toward her. 'Zat is our great aunt Gertrude.' He shuffled over.

I watched until they were deep in conversation.

'Now,' I said. **'Switch it now.'**

'OK.' Piper reached into her pocket. 'Here goes.'

She opened the case on the mantelpiece and placed her egg on the little stand inside.

We looked at it.

'Twist it round a bit,' I said.

She did.

'That's better,' Thomas said.

213

Better? Well, it was better than Little Baby Jesus, I supposed, but not much.

'It looks great, Piper. We'll definitely get away with it,' Thomas said. 'Here you go, Ollie.' He handed me the egg.

I shoved it into my pantaloon pocket.

Then I waited till Leo wasn't looking and gave Grandma a nod.

'We mustn't outstay our welcome.' Grandma bustled up. 'Let's get ourselves together, children.'

'Good idea,' I said. I picked up Rose and started heading for the door.

'It's been a pleasure,' Leo said. 'If you are effer out this way again, you must call in. I vud love to see my young friend dance again.'

Blimey. I wouldn't.

'Thank you for allowing me to see the egg,' Thomas said. 'I've put it back.'

'How kind,' Leo said. 'I vill just go and lock the case.'

'Let me,' said Thomas.

'No, no.' Leo waved him aside and headed for the mantelpiece.

I held my breath.

Piper shut her eyes.

Rose suddenly started scrabbling. I tried to hang on to him, but I couldn't.

He **leapt** from my arms.

I tried to grab him, but I wasn't fast enough.

He zigzagged across the room like a mad thing, yapping his head off. Then he swerved back, straight across Leo's path.

LEO TRIPPED.

He didn't fall, as he managed to grab the edge of the table, but his glasses went flying.

Grandma raced over. **'Leo,'** she screeched. **'Are you all right?'**

There was a <u>**CRUNCH**</u>.

'Oh dear,' Grandma looked down. 'I stepped on your spectacles.'

She picked them up. 'I am SO sorry. Have you got

any others?'

'Yes, yes, I have plenty.' Leo popped his broken glasses back on and peered about. 'Zey are not too bad,' he said. 'I will see you to the door and then I vill go and find another pair.'

I couldn't believe our luck. **He had forgotten about locking the case!**

Grandma apologised all the way to the front door. 'I'm sure your glasses are fixable,' she kept saying. 'I don't know what came over Rose. Perhaps he saw a mouse? Are there mice?'

Rose looked rather pleased with himself, if you asked me.

'Many thanks for the tea,' Thomas said. 'And for showing us the egg.'

'It vos my pleasure,' Leo said. 'I hope you vill come again?'

'Oh yes.' Grandma nodded enthusiastically.

'I have called for ze car,' Leo said. 'Karl is bringing it round.'

We were just about to go outside when a phone rang. It was one of those old-fashioned ones, attached to the wall.

217

'Von minute.' Leo raced over and picked up the receiver.

''Ello?' he said.

And then he said, 'Who?'

And then he said, 'No, that cannot be,' and turned to glare at us.

'Perhaps we should make a move,' Piper muttered.

'An excellent idea,' said Thomas.

I started edging towards the door.

Leo put the receiver down.

He didn't look very happy.

'Anything important?' Grandma asked. She started edging too.

I could see Karl waiting on the driveway. The engine was running.

'We really should go,' Piper said. 'We're letting all your heat out.'

'Vait,' Leo said. 'That vos a call from a person I have not seen for a long, long while.'

'Really?' Thomas sounded nervous.

'Yes,' Leo said. 'And zey said something strange.'

'What?' Grandma tucked Rose under her coat.

Leo glared at her. 'Zey said, you have swapped ze eggs. That you haf taken mine and left an inferior one in its place.'

'Rubbish,' Grandma said. 'Absolutely not. We don't have your egg. Go and have a look. We never swapped it. Come on, children. Hats on. Time to go.' She hustled us towards the door. 'Head for the car,' she muttered.

'STOP.' Leo stamped his foot. 'If you haf my egg, you must gif it back. If you do not, I vill call ze politsiya.'

'No you won't,' Grandma said. 'Because you stole the egg yourself. **Ha!**' She picked up her skirts. 'Come on, children. We must escape from the nasty egg thief.' She hurtled out the door.

Piper and Thomas sprinted after her.

Leo was quite nimble for someone who looked so old. He grabbed at the sleeve of my blouse but

I managed to dodge him. I charged down the path after the others.

'You vill not get away with this,' Leo raged.

I glanced behind. He was after me – but I was faster. Eh? What was he doing? He'd suddenly swerved off to the right.

Oh no! He was heading for the snowmobiles! He'd catch up with us in seconds on one of those. I looked up the path. Karl hadn't realised what was going on. He was still holding the passenger door open.

'I bet that was Edna on the phone,' puffed Grandma, as I caught up. 'She's the only one who knew about the egg swapping.'

'We really need to hurry, Grandma,' I said. 'Seriously.' I glanced behind again.

Leo was perched on a snowmobile and revving up the engine. As I watched he took off in a spray of snow. **He was heading straight for us!**

'Did you have a nice night?' Karl asked as I threw myself past him on to the back seat.

'Excellent, thanks,' I said as Thomas and Piper dived in after me.

We waited for Grandma to follow, but the car door slammed shut. Where was she? Had Leo got her??

The glass partition shot back.

'Right. Where to?'

Eh?

GRANDMA WAS IN THE DRIVER'S SEAT!

She revved the car loudly. 'Belts on.' She slammed the car into gear. 'Hold tight. We're off.'

'WATCH THE FOUNTAIN,' shrieked Piper.

We missed it by a whisker.

Grandma spun the wheel and we speeded up the drive.

'Where's Karl?' I asked.

Thomas looked out of the back window. 'Is that him in the snowdrift?'

'He slipped,' Grandma said.

'Really?' Piper said.

'Yes. Just after he said I could borrow the car. He said, "Take the car with my blessing. You are doing a fine thing."'

'Did he?' I said.

Grandma shrugged. 'Well, he said something. It was in Russian, so it could have been that.'

I could see a bright light in the rear-view mirror. It was coming up behind us surprisingly fast.

'Grandma,' I said. 'Leo's after us.'

'I know,' Grandma said. 'Don't worry. We'll soon shake him off.' She dropped a gear and pushed her foot to the floor.

I covered my eyes.

Thomas chortled with excitement. 'This is just the best fun,' he said. 'Go faster.'

I looked at Thomas. If this was him being less good, I think I preferred him before.

The gates loomed ahead, lit up against the sky.

'Grandma,' I said in a panic. **'They're shut!'**

'They're automatic,' Grandma said. 'They'll open in a minute, you'll see.'

She drove straight at them.

OMG. They were still shut.

I braced for impact.

'Maybe not.' Grandma wrenched the wheel to the right.

'WOOHOO,' shouted Piper. 'Where are we going?'

'We'll take the scenic route,' Grandma said. 'Hang on, it might be bumpy.'

It was. **Very.** We jolted along through pine trees and parkland. The car was skidding everywhere.

'Do you know where we're going?' I asked.

'Yes.' Grandma zigzagged through some trees.

'Almost there.'

How we could be? We were in a wood.

I leant forward and tried to see. The headlights lit up the snow that had started to fall, and … what was that? Was that a road? A main one? Yes! It must be! I could see buildings and street lights.

Thank goodness. We'd be back at the museum in no time.

'Right,' Grandma said. 'Keep an eye out. We need to find a slipway.'

'Slipway?' Thomas blinked. 'You mean the thing boats go down? Into water?'

'Yes,' Grandma said, gaily. 'That's right. A slipway.'

Piper and I looked at each other in horror.

'We're going into water?' I said.

I peered out the window again. OMG. What I'd seen wasn't a road. It was the river.

'Don't panic,' Grandma said. 'It's frozen. Thomas himself said you could drive a bus along it. It's the fastest way back to the museum. No traffic. Ah.' She spun the wheel. 'Here we go.'

She speeded up.

I stared at Thomas. 'Tell her to stop,' I said. 'We'll drown.'

'Too late.' Thomas clapped his hands. "Wheeeeeeeee!"

We shot down the slipway and hurtled on to the ice. We spun, round and round. OMG. We were almost at the far side. We were going to hit the post!

THWACK.

The rear bumper caught it and we started spinning in the opposite direction.

'**Woo!**' yelled Thomas. 'Well done, Florence!'

I shut my eyes and held on to Rose for dear life. The ice would crack any minute. We'd plummet into the icy depths and perish horribly. No one would ever know what had happened to us. Mum would be ringing the study centre in Suffolk. 'Two small boys?' she'd say. 'And a ginger girl?' We'd neve—

'Are you OK, Ollie?' Piper said.

Oh. Had we stopped spinning? I opened one eye and then the other. Yes, we had. Rose was looking annoyed. I'd probably squashed him.

'Fine,' I said. 'Are we off the ice yet?'

'No.' Grandma slammed the car into first gear. **'Hold on.'**

Grandma couldn't go as fast as she wanted, as the ice was so slippery. Every time she tried to accelerate, we started to skid.

She was doing a lot of muttering and quite a bit of it was rude.

I turned and looked out of the back window. I could see a light.

'Leo's behind us again,' I said. 'You need to go **faster.**'

Grandma put her foot down.

We spun in a large circle.

'It's not like this in the films,' she said crossly. 'Never mind. The museum's just up here on the right. Look for a way off.'

'There,' Piper shouted. 'Another slipway.'

It was steep and covered in snow.

'We'll never get up that,' I said.

'We will if we go fast enough,' Thomas said.

'Hang on.' Grandma pulled on the handbrake and swung the car around. 'We'll go up in reverse. More traction.'

The wheels squealed.

I closed my eyes again. Slush flew past the windows.

'Woohoo!' Thomas shouted.

I buried my face in Rose's fur.

There was a **CRUNCH**.

My eyes flew open.

'Just a lamp post,' said Grandma. 'We're back on the street.'

She indicated and pulled out.

She drove sedately along. 'Look casual, everyone,' she said.

'Are you all right, Ollie?' Piper asked me. 'You look a bit green.'

'I enjoyed every minute,' I lied.

'So did I.' Thomas gave a little bounce.

'Any sign of Leo?' Grandma asked.

We turned and looked.

'No,' I said. 'I think we lost him.'

Grandma swung into a side street and screeched to a halt. 'We'll walk the rest of the way,' she said. 'Stay in the shadows, just in case.'

'Won't Leo know where we're heading?' Piper jumped out of the car. 'Karl picked us up from the museum earlier.'

Grandma rolled her eyes. 'If we were staying at the museum, Piper, we would have asked to be picked up from somewhere else.'

'But we are,' I said.

'Are what?'

'Staying at the museum,' I said.

'Exactly,' Grandma said. 'This way.' She took us round the back. 'There's a service door,' she said.

'Won't it be locked?' Piper asked.

'Of course.' Grandma rummaged in her bag. 'Ah.

Here they are.' She pulled out a huge bunch of keys.

'Where did you get those?' I asked.

'Viktor's desk. He lent them to me.' She stuck one in the lock. 'Well, he **would** have done, I'm sure, if I'd asked.'

'But you didn't?' Piper asked. 'Ask?'

'I fully intended to, Piper, but it slipped my mind.' Grandma pushed the door. 'Wonderful. We're in.'

We clattered through.

'Excuse me.' Thomas put his hand up. 'But if returning the egg is a surprise, shouldn't we be quiet?'

'Oh, yes. I forgot. Tippy-toes, everyone,' Grandma bellowed. 'Where's the light?' She felt about inside the door.

'Why don't we use a torch?' I said. 'If we're trying to be inconspicuous?'

'I've got one.' Piper pulled it from her coat and switched it on. 'Which way?'

'Straight on,' said Grandma. 'Along the passage.

Then second right.'

There wasn't a second right, so we went left instead. And then we took a right, and two more lefts, and then we came back to where we'd come in.

We did that **twice**, and Grandma got cross and blamed everyone for being rubbish at directions, but then Piper found some stairs so we went up those.

They came out in the kitchens. All the lights were off, but moonlight streamed in.

Piper switched her torch off. 'It's very quiet,' she said. 'Where do you think Viktor is?'

We crept into the main hall and listened at the foot of the stairs.

Nothing.

'Maybe he took Edna to dinner?' Thomas said.

'Do you really think it was her who called Leo?' I asked.

'It must have been,' Grandma huffed. 'No one else knew our plan. What a meanie, trying to get us in trouble like that.'

'It doesn't matter,' Piper said. 'We've got the real Moscow Star! How amazing is that? Let's put it back, and then find Viktor. He'll be over the moon.'

'You're right.' Grandma looked cheerful again. 'This time tomorrow we'll be eating cake at the Kremlin! Have you got it, Ollie?'

I patted my pantaloons. 'I certainly have,' I said.

'Someone has to switch the power off again,' Piper said. 'So we can open the cabinet and swap it over.'

'I'll do it,' said Thomas. 'Can I take the torch?'

Piper handed it to him. 'Give us a few minutes to get upstairs,' she said.

'OK,' said Thomas.

'Don't get locked in, will you?' I said.

Thomas looked at me. 'Who would be so stupid?' he said.

31

We headed for the egg room.

I took the Moscow Star out of my pocket. It really was beautiful. I wasn't surprised Leo had wanted it so badly.

Grandma stopped. 'You can put it back, Ollie,' she said. 'It's dark in there. You'll have to feel your way. It'll be good for your explorer genes.'

'OK,' I said. 'Thanks.'

I tiptoed in and **immediately** tripped over Viktor's mop bucket. He'd left it practically in the doorway. I'd almost dropped the egg!

Honestly. You'd have thought he'd have put it away.

'You're making a lot of noise,' Piper said.

'Sorry.' I took a few more steps. It was no good. 'I can't see anything,' I complained. 'I'll have to switch the light on to get my bearings.'

Grandma tutted. 'If you must,' she said.

I turned back towards the door.

Then I tripped again. Over the edge of a rug this time.

The Moscow Star went flying.

There was a splash.

'Ollie?' Piper found the light switch. 'What was that?'

'Nothing.' I scrambled to my feet and dashed over to the bucket. Phew. There it was, sitting in the mop water.

'You never dropped the egg?' Grandma screeched.

I fished it out and held it up. 'It's fine.'

'Thank goodness for that.' Grandma mopped her brow. 'Triumphantly returning a priceless stolen

234

artefact wouldn't be nearly as good if it was in bits.'

'It's just a bit wet.' I looked around for something to dry it with.

'Here,' Piper said. 'I'll use my sleeve. It's quite floaty.'

She took the egg and started to pat it dry.

Then she stopped.

'What?' I asked. 'Why are you looking like that?'

Piper didn't say anything. She just held the egg out.

OMG. Half the stars were missing.

'What did you do?' I stared at her.

'They just fell off,' Piper said.

Grandma dashed over. 'They can't have just fallen off,' she said. 'Fabergé's work was built to last!'

'The water must have dissolved the glue,' I said.

We all stood and looked at the ruined egg.

'It's not a Fabergé, is it?' Piper said, sadly. **'It's a fake.'** She picked another gem off. 'There won't be a reward for returning a copy.'

'It's a very good copy, though,' Grandma said. 'It's every bit as good as the one Edna made for me.' She paused. 'Well, it was before you dropped it in the mop bucket, Ollie.'

'I don't understand,' I said. 'Did Leo steal a fake egg from the museum?'

Grandma shrugged. 'It looks like it.'

'In that case,' Piper said, 'where's the **real** Moscow Star?'

'Maybe it's the one in the cabinet?' I started walking over. 'Perhaps it's not a copy after all?'

Grandma snorted. 'Of course it's a copy. Why would Victor say it had been stolen if it hadn't?'

'We could check it,' Piper said. 'With the metal detector.'

'We could.' I peered into the cabinet. 'If it was there.'

'What do you mean?' Grandma squawked.

'It's gone,' I said.

'Gone?' Piper raced over. 'But you put it back,

didn't you?'

'Of course I did,' I said.

'Are you sure, Ollie?' Grandma pushed me out of the way and squinted through the glass. 'Because there's definitely nothing there.'

Grandma didn't get to hear my further thoughts on the matter, as a voice bellowed at us from the doorway.

'Vere, you varmints, is my egg?'

Bum. It was Leo.

32

Leo looked ever so cross. 'Vere is it?' He shook his fist. 'I vont my egg.'

'It's here.' Grandma threw it. 'Catch.'

He grabbed at it. 'Thank you. Ze cheek of it. Inviting yourself for tea and pinching zis. And ze car!'

'Karl said we could borrow that,' said Grandma. 'I don't know what he told you, but he said he was more than happy for us to drive ourselves.'

'Yes, he definitely did.' Piper nodded in agreement.

'And you have your egg back,' Grandma said. 'I have no idea why you're making so much fuss.'

Leo wasn't listening. He squinted down through his broken glasses. 'Vot happened to it?' He sounded horrified.

'Sorry,' I said. 'I dropped it in the mop bucket.'

'Didn't you know it was a fake?' Piper said.

Leo looked bewildered. 'A fake?' He prodded the egg and then looked at the gems which stuck to his finger. 'No,' he muttered. **'It cannot be.'**

'Serves you right,' Grandma tutted. 'Taking stuff that doesn't belong to you.'

Leo's eyebrows shot into his hair. **'You took zis!'** He held up the egg. **'And now look at it.'**

'I *exchanged* it,' Grandma said. 'You **stole** it!'

'I did not steal it,' Leo said.

'Rubbish.' Grandma headed out of the door. 'I shall fetch Viktor and he can deal with you.'

'Wait!' Leo said. 'Do not go. I vill tell you everything.'

Grandma swung around. 'Will you tell us where the **real** egg is?'

Leo wrung his hands. 'I cannot tell you vot I do not know. I thought zis was ze real egg.'

'It still counts as stealing, you know,' Piper said. 'If you thought it was real when you stole it.'

'I did NOT steal it,' Leo said.

I was getting confused. '**Someone** must have stolen it,' I said.

'It was Viktor,' Leo said. 'Viktor gave me ze Moscow Star.'

'Rubbish,' Grandma said. 'Why would Viktor give you the **most valuable** egg in his collection – and then tell everyone it had been stolen?'

'You must listen,' Leo said. 'Thirty years ago I vos working hard, building my cheesy empire. I came here every day. The museum was peaceful. Oh, I loved the eggs, especially the Moscow Star.' He looked sadly at the soggy mess in his hands.

'So, what happened?' Piper asked.

Leo took his glasses off, and rubbed his eyes. 'Vell,' he said. 'One day, I came here and the museum was cold. Very cold. Viktor was distressed. He said he did not haf enough money to pay for ze heating. He said the museum vud have to close!'

'Oh poor, poor, Viktor.' Grandma dabbed her eye.

Leo nodded. 'I felt sorry for him. I asked if zere

was anything I could do. Donate some cheesy snacks, maybe? But he was not interested in my snacks. He vonted my money!'

'So did you give him some?' Grandma asked.

'Vell, no,' Leo admitted. 'I vos young in those days, and greedy. I said he could have as many cheesy snacks as he liked, but I would not give money unless I had something in return. Then I vent home.'

'That was a bit mean,' said Piper. 'You had **millions!**'

Leo hung his head. 'I feel bad.'

'So you should,' said Grandma, reprovingly.

'Zen,' Leo exclaimed, 'I heard the Moscow Star had been stolen! I vos devastated.'

Grandma rolled her eyes.

'Eet is true! But then, ze next day, Viktor came to my house. He had ze Moscow Star with him! He put it on ze table and let me look at it for a while. Then he said, if I gave him twenty million roubles, he vud let me keep it.'

241

'So you said yes?' Piper said.

'Viktor asked me to think of the museum. He had bills to pay. He said I would be doing a good thing. I let him persuade me.' Leo hung his head. 'I knew it vos wrong. But it vos so beautiful. I said yes before I could stop myself.'

'Blimey,' I said.

Leo went on. 'I felt bad very soon after, and went to tell Viktor that I had changed my mind. But he said it was too late. He said if I did not keep quiet, he vud tell the politsiya I had taken it.' He dabbed his eye. 'My aunt was ze chief at the time. She vos very scary.'

'Aunts generally are,' Grandma agreed.

'And zen,' Leo looked outraged, 'I found out he was **lying** about ze heating bills. He had plenty of money to pay them. He vonted my money to spend on holidays in ze sun!' He shook his head. 'I did not vont to go to prison. I decided I would take good care of ze egg and return it when ze time was right. I did not know I had ze fake. It serves me right.'

Grandma harrumphed. 'So, if what you say is true, **where is the real Moscow Star?**'

Leo shrugged. 'Maybe it vos stolen long, long ago? Maybe Viktor did not even know he was selling me a fake? It was a very good copy, until it fell in zat bucket.'

'Very well.' Grandma grabbed his arm. 'Let's go and find him.' She marched Leo towards the door. 'And then I shall work out which of you is lying.'

Piper and I went to collect Thomas. I was a bit worried, to be honest. The electricity hadn't gone off yet. I hoped he was all right – not electrocuted or anything.

'Where do you think he is?' I asked, as we ran down the stairs.

'He probably forgot the code,' Piper said. She sounded fed up.

'What's wrong?' I asked.

'We can't claim a reward for a fake egg,' she said. 'I'll **never** be able to buy your gran's balloon now.' She jumped down the last step. 'Or a caravan.'

'Do you think Leo's telling the truth about Viktor?' I asked.

'I don't know.' Piper shrugged. 'Leo's egg's a fake, and now the copy in the egg room has disappeared. I'm very confused. Right.' She stopped and looked around.

'Where's he gone?'

Thomas wasn't in the entrance hall, but the basement door was ajar. I stuck my head round. 'Hello?' I called.

There wasn't a reply.

'Thomas?' Piper shouted.

Nothing.

'Is there a light?' Piper asked.

'Broken,' I said. I started to feel my way down.

Piper followed, close behind.

Eh? What was that?

I'd kicked something off the bottom step. Whatever it was clattered, and then rolled. I knelt and groped around until I found it.

'It's your torch, Piper.'

'So he was definitely here.' She sounded worried.

'Yep.' I switched it on and shone it down the passage. I could see the fuse box, but no Thomas.

I hoped he was OK.

'What's behind that door?' Piper tiptoed towards it.

'A workshop,' I said.

'I heard something.' Piper grabbed my arm. **'There's someone in there.'**

We stood still, and listened.

There was a noise. A strange one. A humming, clanking noise.

I pushed gently at the door.

It swung open. Just a tiny bit.

I peered round.

Oh. It wasn't Thomas.

'It's Edna,' I whispered.

She was sitting at the workbench, with her back to me. In front of her, whirring away, was the copier from Viktor's office.

Next to that was an open packet of teacakes, and a basket, filled to the brim with glittering eggs.

Copies of the Moscow Star.

'What's she doing?' Piper whispered back.

I pushed the door a little more, so she could see.

Her mouth dropped open. 'Blimey,' she said.

She was so surprised she fell against the door, and we both crashed into the room.

OW.

Edna spun around. She scowled when she saw us. **'Oi,'** she said. 'You're not supposed to be here.'

I scrambled to my feet. 'What are you doing?' I asked.

'What does it **look** like?' Edna sounded annoyed. She turned back to the workbench. 'I'm working.'

'Are those for Viktor?' I asked.

'Yep.' Edna picked up a star and glued it on an egg. 'Good, aren't they? This machine's top. I popped in the egg from upstairs – and it's knocking out copies like there's no tomorrow.' She pointed to the basket.

'All I have to do is paint them, and glue on the stars.'

'They're amazing.' Piper got up. 'Are there any spares? It's Mum's birthday soon.'

Edna sniggered. 'I expect Viktor would sell you one. Last time he charged twenty million roubles.'

'What do you mean, *last time*?' Piper said.

Edna looked flustered. **'Nothing,'** she said. **'I didn't say anything.'**

'Yes you did,' I said. 'Come on. You may as well tell us.'

'Can't.' Edna concentrated on a fiddly bit.

'You're almost out of teacakes.' Piper waved the packet. 'I'll get you some more.'

Edna wavered. She put her paintbrush down. 'Nice ones? From the bakery on the corner?'

'As many as you like,' promised Piper.

Edna shrugged. 'OK then. I'll tell you. Don't mention it to Viktor. He might grass me up to the Royal Society of Replicators. I could lose my licence.'

'You can trust us.' Piper did her best to look trustworthy.

'I was just starting out,' Edna said. 'I met Viktor at an exhibition. When I said what I did, he ordered four copies of the Moscow Star.'

'Did he say why he wanted them?' I asked.

'I didn't ask,' Edna said, quickly. 'You're not supposed to. It's in the rules.'

'Really?' Piper raised an eyebrow. 'I'd have asked.'

Edna snorted. 'I didn't need to. Viktor couldn't wait to tell me about his "amazing idea". He wanted money. Real money, to spend on holidays. He knew loads of billionaires who'd do anything to get their hands on a Fabergé. The Moscow Star was the easiest to copy, because it didn't open. We wouldn't have to replicate the inside.'

'Wow.' Piper looked impressed. 'Good thinking.'

'He reported the Moscow Star as stolen, then offered the copies for sale, **pretending** they were the real thing.' Edna flicked a sequin across the bench. 'He spun them a sob story. Said he needed to pay for heating. Made them feel better about buying stolen goods.'

'So they all thought they had the real egg,' Piper said. 'Including Leo.'

'Yep. What a load of twits.' Edna sniggered. She nodded towards the basket. 'I expect he'll do the same with those.'

'Blimey.' Piper looked at the pile of eggs. 'You'll be rich.'

Edna shook her head. 'I get an hourly rate,' she said. 'I'm not in it for the money.'

'Not in it for the money?' Piper looked bewildered. 'What are you in it for, then?' she asked.

Edna deftly picked up a gem with some tiny tweezers. **'REVENGE.'**

'Revenge?' I blinked. 'On who?'

Edna concentrated hard on her egg.

'We're happy to listen,' Piper said, kindly. 'Have the last teacake.'

'Ta.' Edna put the tweezers down and took it. She reached for a knife. 'I was an artist once,' she said. 'A proper one. My paintings of kittens in baskets were second to none.'

'You're very talented.' Piper patted her arm. 'I'm sure they were beautiful.'

'Yes.' Edna slapped butter on the teacake. 'They were.' She slammed the two halves together. 'Everyone said so.'

A vein had started to pulse in her forehead.

I took a step backwards.

'One year, in London, there was an exhibition. All the great artists submitted their work. I spent months on my picture. **Months**.'

'What happened?' Piper asked.

'They rejected it.' Edna jumped to her feet, her bristles twitching. 'They rejected it in favour of a modern work involving locusts, giraffe poo and a small electric train.'

'Gracious.' Piper blinked. 'That's ... that's terrible.'

'Yes, it was.' Edna was purple now. 'What do curators know? <u>**NOTHING**</u>.' She smashed the teacake into the bench. 'I vowed I would not rest until I had a work hanging in every major gallery in the world.'

She stood there, breathing heavily.

'By work,' Piper said, delicately, 'you mean forgery?'

'Yes.' Edna looked triumphant. 'Exactly that. I've only got two to go.'

'Really?' I said. 'That's impressive.'

'Miserable old **gits**.' Edna stabbed a currant with the end of her finger. 'When they discover the truth, they'll look like right ninnies.'

'The truth that their most famous works are fakes?'

'Yep.' Edna guffawed.

Blimey. I blinked. Edna was actually a little bit nuts.

'What do you do with the real artworks?' Piper asked. 'Once you've replaced them?'

Edna shrugged. 'Charity shops, mostly.'

I looked at her. 'Did you tell Viktor Grandma's

plan? About the egg swap?'

Edna hung her head. 'Sorry. It slipped out. He thought it was hilarious. Your gran was planning to switch a fake for a fake.'

'So it was him that phoned Leo? Not you?'

'I expect he was hoping Leo would get rid of you.' Edna tapped the table. 'Are you going to get me any more teacakes or not?'

'One last question,' Piper said. 'Where's the real Moscow Star? Is it the one that's been in the egg room all along?'

'Hang on. I'll have a look.' Edna reached into the top of the copier and fished out an egg. She inspected it closely. 'Looks like a copy to me.' She chucked it on top of the others. 'I expect Viktor's got the real one hidden somewhere.'

'Where is Viktor?' I asked.

'Viktor? He took your friend up to the roof.'

I looked at her in horror. **Thomas?**

'Small boy? Waistcoat? Tampering with the

electrics? Sneezed at a rat and gave himself away?'

'That's him.' I grabbed Piper by the arm. **'Come on. Quick!'**

'You'd better hurry,' Edna called after us. 'Viktor said something about your gran's balloon.'

34

We raced as fast as we could up the stairs and along the corridor with all the chandeliers.

'I hope we're in time,' Piper said.

'So do I,' I said. 'Mum will be **furious** if we go back without him.'

Luckily Viktor hadn't locked any of the doors, so we belted through them and up the final flight of stairs to the roof.

We burst out into the icy air.

'Oh no,' I said.

Grandma's balloon was almost fully inflated. The basket already bobbed a foot or two from the ground.

'There's Viktor.' Piper pointed. 'He's untying the mooring rope.' She started to run. **'Come on. We have to stop him!'**

Viktor must have heard her shout. He dropped the

rope and turned to face us.

He was wearing his hat and his fur cloak was billowing in the wind. He looked huge, and **very scary**.

I reminded myself of his tiny bald head.

'What should we do?' muttered Piper.

I wasn't sure. Even though there were two of us, we couldn't tackle him. We'd have to use our wits.

He stepped forward as we approached, but he didn't say anything.

He just looked at us.

My wits didn't make an appearance. I'd have to wing it.

'Hi, Viktor.' I beamed at him. 'We left our toothbrushes in the basket.

Grandma sent us to get them.'

'Is that so?' Viktor said. 'Go on then.'

He bent down and picked up the rope again.

'Um, you're not going to untie that while we're on board, are you?' I said, nervously.

'Wouldn't dream of it.' Viktor carried on tugging at the knot.

A muffled yell drifted over.

'Gracious.' Piper looked around. 'Who could that be?'

'Your friend. He's perfectly fine.' Viktor smirked. 'He forgot his toothbrush too.'

'What shall we do?' I muttered to Piper. 'We need to stall him.'

Piper took a step. 'We know about the Moscow Star,' she said. 'And how you sold it. More than once.'

'Do you now?' Viktor swung round. He didn't look very pleased.

'It was a **great idea**,' Piper said. She gave me a nudge.

'Yes. **Really clever**,' I said. 'You must have

made an awful lot of money.'

'Oh yes.' Viktor nodded. 'All those wealthy people, desperate to own something no one else had.' He giggled. 'Not one realised they had a fake.'

'Edna's very good,' Piper said. 'Amazing workmanship.'

'Incredible,' Viktor said. 'She's replicating some more for me now, actually.'

'Why?' I said. 'Didn't you make millions with the first batch?'

Viktor sighed. 'It's amazing how quickly money runs out. Once I'd bought myself a small Caribbean island, the coffers were practically empty. I needed some more to retire on.' He giggled. 'And then you lot turned up. When it turned out that Edna was just down the road I couldn't believe my luck. Such an opportunity.'

I looked at him. 'And we rescued her for you.'

'Yes. Thank you.' Viktor bowed. 'I tried to make it easy.'

'You told Ollie's gran about the job,' Piper said.

'Sometimes I amaze myself with my **brilliance**.' Viktor preened. 'I gave her the advert, and ⓑⓘⓝⓖⓞ!'

'And Anya?' I said. 'She was in the photo on your desk.'

'My sister,' Viktor said. 'Her name's Tracy, actually, but I suggested she change it in case you got suspicious. I told her Edna was a friend of mine, and completely innocent. She was happy to help. The job was yours before you even left the museum.'

I felt a bit miffed. I thought I'd peformed really well in that interview.

'I asked her to leave you the key and put senna pods in the spice jar.' Viktor gave a little snort. 'I hear that worked well?'

'Very,' I said.

'She was so helpful. She even altered Edna's prison records.' Viktor rubbed his hands in glee. 'Edna McAngelo. Released without charge. I did not want the politsiya turning up before her work was done.'

So that was why no one had come after us. I'd just thought we were lucky.

'You had the Moscow Star all along,' Piper said 'Where is it?'

Viktor turned back to the rope. 'I'm not telling you that. I'm keeping it for myself.'

Piper shook her head. 'But if you sell all the copies, you'll be rich. Why not leave the real one in the museum? Where it belongs?'

Viktor stared at her. **'Because inside the Moscow Star is an emerald the size of a pigeon's egg.** I've been working on the combination for years. One day I'll get it right, and the emerald will be mine.' He gave a little giggle. 'It will make up for my childhood of poverty.'

'You weren't that poor,' I said. 'You just didn't have a pony.'

'It's not like you had to share a bedroom.' Piper glared at him.

'OOMPH.' A shout came from the balloon.

'Ah.' Viktor blinked. 'Your friend. He hasn't managed to find his toothbrush. Perhaps you should go and help him?'

I looked at the knot in Viktor's hands. It was almost undone. If we left it any longer, Thomas would be heading for the Baltic.

We didn't have a choice.

'Come on, Piper,' I said. **'Run.'**

35

Piper got to the basket just ahead of me. She scrambled over the edge then turned to pull me in.

There was Thomas. All trussed up at the bottom.

'Mffff,' he said.

Piper pulled the tape from his mouth.

'Viktor,' Thomas shouted. **'Viktor. He's the thief. He stole the Moscow Star.'**

'We know,' Piper said.

'Oh,' said Thomas.

The balloon gave a lurch.

'Can you fly this thing, Ollie?' Piper looked up.

'I can have a go,' I said.

'It won't work.' Thomas tried to wriggle free. 'Viktor unscrewed something from the engine. It's in his pocket.'

I started to panic. We didn't have long.

'We haven't got time to untie you, Thomas,' I said. 'Take his feet, Piper.'

Piper grabbed them.

'Hey,' Thomas squawked. 'Careful.'

Blimey. He was ever so heavy. Even so, I managed to heave him up on to the rim of the basket while Piper shoved from below.

'It's too far down to roll him off the edge,' I said to Piper. 'We'll have to lower him.'

'OK.' Piper grabbed a cable to pull herself up. There was a whoosh, and the balloon gave a lurch.

I grabbed Thomas. 'That's the burner handle, Piper.'

'Oops. Sorry.' She let go, but it was too late. We'd risen another few feet. There was no way we could lower Thomas safely now. Viktor was below us, over in the shadows. He'd given up on my knot and taken out a penknife. **We were out of time.**

Piper looked at me. 'What shall we do?' she asked.

'I know.' Thomas stuck his head up. 'Take my

arms and legs. Swing me!'

I peered down at the icy concrete. 'Won't that hurt?'

Thomas didn't look worried. **'Aim for Viktor!'**

'Yay.' Piper scrambled on to the edge and grabbed Thomas's feet. 'Come on, Ollie.'

I took Thomas's wrists. 'Ready?' I shouted. 'One. Two. Threeeeeeeeee!'

Thomas soared through the air. He hit Viktor squarely in the back.

Viktor flew **headfirst** into a pile of snow.

'Yay!' shouted Piper. **'Got him!'**

We jumped down and dashed over to Thomas.

'Are you OK?' I asked. 'We'll carry you.'

'I'm fine. My legs are almost free.' Thomas struggled to his feet. 'The string snapped.' He bent down to free himself.

'Thomas! We need to run.' Piper grabbed his arm.

Too late. Viktor had struggled out of the snowdrift. He stormed towards us.

'Leave me,' Thomas shouted. **'Save yourselves.'**

There wasn't time to save anything. Viktor was seething. He grabbed my blouse with one hand and Piper's with the other and pushed us towards the balloon.

I tried to pull away, but I couldn't. 'Grandma will be here any minute,' I said. 'She's bound to come and look for us.'

'I hope she can swim.' Viktor narrowed his eyes. 'Because by the time she turns up, you three will be in the Baltic, **wrestling with sharks.**'

'I think we've established there are no sharks in the Baltic, actually,' I said.

'Hey,' Piper said. 'Look at Thomas!'

265

I looked. 'Why's he spinning like that?'

Victor saw our faces and turned. 'What's he doing?' he said. He sounded nervous.

'I think he's ... pirouetting?' Piper said.

Wow.

Thomas spun towards us over the ice, faster and faster, until he was just a blur.

Then, still spinning, **he made a mighty leap.**

His feet hit Viktor in the chest.

Viktor didn't stand a chance. He went over like a ninepin.

Thomas spun off into a pile of snow.

Piper and I sat on Viktor, but only for about two seconds, because then he pushed us off and made a dash for it.

He **vaulted** into the basket.

'What's he doing?' I said. 'He can't go anywhere. It's still tied to that post.'

Just as I said that, there was a huge gust of wind. The rope pulled taut, and the last few strands gave way.

The balloon shot upwards.

Thomas made one last leap, but it was just for show.

There was nothing we could do.

Viktor had escaped.

We found Grandma in Viktor's study, toasting crumpets. I was quite surprised to see Leo there as well. Rose was snoozing on the rug.

'Hi,' I said. 'We found Thomas.'

'I couldn't find Viktor,' Grandma said. 'I looked everywhere. And then I got bored and Leo said he was chilly so I brought him up here. Crumpet?'

'No thanks,' I said. 'Guess what?'

'Ooooh. I love a good guessing game.' Grandma leant forward in her chair. 'Now let me think—'

I decided not to wait. 'Viktor was the one that stole the Moscow Star,' I said.

Grandma's mouth dropped open. **'I knew it,'** she squawked.

'He got Edna to make him four copies,' Piper said. 'Thirty years ago. One was kept in the egg room. He sold the other three.'

Leo jumped to his feet. 'So I vos not the only one?'

'No,' Piper said. 'He made a fortune.'

'I suspected him almost right away.' Grandma slapped the arm of her chair. 'It was his tiny little eyes. Was Edna in on it?'

'Sort of,' I said. 'But not for the money.'

The door flew open.

Oh.

It was Edna.

She waddled in with the basket of Moscow Stars.

'Evening.' Grandma sounded frosty.

'Florence.' Edna gave her a nod. She walked over to Viktor's desk. 'I'll leave these here.'

Piper went over. 'Viktor's gone,' she said. 'You probably won't get paid.'

Edna scowled. 'I never liked him. Did you get the teacakes?'

'Not yet,' Piper said. 'Sorry.'

'Have a crumpet.' Grandma held out the plate.

'I will. Ta.' Edna took one. 'Sorry I didn't make you another egg.'

'Don't worry about it,' Grandma said. 'Do come and visit when you're next in Great Potton.'

'OK,' Edna said. 'Will do.' She stuffed the crumpet in her mouth. 'I'll get going. Big job. Paris. Can't remember what the bloke said. Something to do with Fiona and Lisa.' Her brow furrowed. 'Or was it Shona and Lisa?'

'Brona?' Piper said, helpfully.

'Iona?' Thomas suggested.

'Nope.' Edna shrugged. 'None of those. Whatever. I'm not supposed to say, anyway. **See ya.**'

The door slammed behind her.

'So vere is Viktor?' Leo asked. 'I vud like a word.'

'So would I,' Grandma said. 'I shall make him tell me where the real egg is.'

'He escaped,' I said. 'I'm really sorry. He took your balloon.'

'Did he?' Grandma smirked.

'Aren't you cross?' I said.

'Oh no. Not at all.' She pulled her phone out of her pocket and switched it on. 'He won't get far.'

'Are you ringing the politsiya?' Piper asked.

Grandma tapped the screen. 'Not yet.'

'What then?'

'I've got an app. It's linked to the sat nav.' She held it out. 'See.'

Thomas took it. 'He's heading for the Caribbean.'

'That's where his island is,' I said.

'An island?' Grandma said. 'Oooh, how lovely.' She took the phone back and tapped away. 'Such a shame the balloon's changed direction.' She gave a little giggle. 'I wonder if he'll notice he's circling Poland. He should be back on the museum roof in a hour. I'll give the politsiya a call just before he arrives.'

'HA,' Leo said. 'That vill teach the old crook.'

Piper raised her eyebrows.

Leo looked embarrassed. 'But I am not like Viktor,' he said. 'I am sorry for vot I did. I vill gif lots of money to charity to show my remorse.'

'Good job,' said Piper.

I walked over to Viktor's desk. 'Should we look for the real egg?' I asked.

'Oh yes.' Grandma jumped up and raced across. 'I bet it's in there somewhere.'

Even Rose helped, sniffing away. We turned out every drawer, even the secret ones. Piper waved her metal detector over everything in sight. In the end the batteries ran out.

There was no sign of the Moscow Star.

'It could be anywhere,' I said. I felt really disappointed. Tea at the Kremlin would have been brilliant. I could have written about it in my 'What I

Did in My Holidays' essay. I'd definitely have won.

'Viktor may confess to the politsiya,' Grandma mused.

Piper looked cross. 'I hope he does – otherwise we won't get the reward,' she said. 'And then I won't be able to buy the balloon.'

'Don't worry,' Grandma said. 'I've decided not to sell.'

Piper looked quite put out. 'Have you?' she said.

'Yes.' Grandma nodded. 'I'm keeping it. I'm far too young to retire. I don't know what came over me.'

'Really?' Woohoo! That was the best news ever! I gave her a hug.

'Ollie.'

'What, Grandma?'

'Don't tell your mum. Not yet. She thinks I'm starting at the charity shop on Saturday. I'll break the news gently.'

37

The politsiya arrested Viktor on the roof just before midnight.

He looked very surprised when he peered over the edge of the basket and saw us all standing there. He blinked quite a lot and then he turned around and tried to re-program the sat nav, but Grandma kept tapping her phone and overriding him.

'**I'll tell you where the Moscow Star is,**' he kept shouting as they marched him off. '**It's in my desk. It was only a joke. I was going to put it back.**'

'It's not in his desk,' Piper said bitterly. 'He's such a liar.'

Leo took the fake eggs to auction for good causes. Piper looked disappointed as he carried them off. 'It's a shame we couldn't have kept one,' she said. 'For a souvenir.'

'Actually, Piper,' Grandma said, 'I've just this minute discovered an egg in my bag. **I've no idea how it got there.** Nothing to do with me. It must have accidentally rolled in.' She rummaged around and pulled it out. 'Here it is.'

'It rolled in by accident?' I looked at her suspiciously.

'It must have done,' Grandma said. 'There's a whole load of humbugs in there as well. No idea where they came from either. **Bizarre**.'

'I tipped the humbugs in,' I said. 'So we could use the tin.'

'Ah, I see.' Grandma handed Piper the egg. 'There you go,' she said. 'Your very own Moscow Star.'

Piper was thrilled. 'Thanks, Ollie's gran. Are you sure?'

'Of course,' Grandma said. 'Just don't get it wet.'

Mum was quite surprised to see us the next day. She hadn't been expecting us back till Thursday.

She looked at my pantaloons. 'What on **earth** are you wearing?'

Grandma told her there'd been a flood, right in the middle of a drama workshop, and we'd had to evacuate. 'Such a shame,' she said.

Mum looked a bit suspicious, but she didn't ask any more questions.

'Oh,' she said. 'Thomas. There was a call for you earlier.'

'Was there?' Thomas looked surprised.

'Yes. A lady with an accent.' Mum looked around. 'I wrote her name down somewhere. She wants you to call her back.'

Blimey. It turned out that Leo had recommended Thomas to the principal of the St Petersburg School of Dance.

They'd only offered him a place.

According to Thomas, it's the best ballet school in the world.

'Will your parents let you go?' Piper asked.

'Oh yes.' Thomas gave a little twirl. 'I've already asked. Mum's thrilled I'm good at something other than pottery. She'll be able to boast properly from now on.'

Grandma got a call from Russia as well, but hers was from the politsiya.

'They've deported Viktor,' she said. 'He's back in Essex. Litter picking on Canvey Island.'

'Well, he did want to retire to an island,' Piper said.

'Have they found the Moscow Star yet?' I asked.

'No,' Grandma mused. 'Viktor insists it was in his desk, and says someone must have taken it.'

'It's annoying,' Piper said. 'I could have done with the reward, even if someone did change their mind about selling stuff.' She gave Grandma a pointed look.

'Oh,' I said. 'About that. You know I said a rouble was worth a pound?'

'Yes,' Piper said.

'It's not.'

'What is it worth then?' She looked at me.

'Just over a penny.'

Piper looked outraged. 'A penny? So twenty-five thousand roubles is—'

'About three hundred pounds,' I said.

Piper stared at me. 'All that effort for three hundred pounds?' she said. **'That we didn't even get?'**

I had to remind her about the worthwhile bit.

I didn't win the 'What I Did in My Holidays' competition. Apparently my essay was too far-fetched!

Thea won it. She only went to **Clacton!**

I went to the park with Piper, and complained. 'Mrs Jones said I had an overactive imagination, and did I know what a fronted adverbial was.'

'You should have shown her the egg,' Piper said. She took it out of her pocket and held it up. It sparkled in the light. 'Do you?'

'Do I what?' I looked at her.

'Know what a fronted adverbial is?'

I felt I should. 'Some kind of newt?'

'No.'

We sat on the bandstand steps, and kept an eye out for the park-keeper, as Piper had brought her metal detector. We'd decided to stick to the 'Gold and Silver' setting from now on. We were fed up with digging up ring-pulls.

'I got you some batteries.' I rummaged in my bag. 'Here you are.'

Piper looked surprised. 'Thanks, Ollie.'

'That's OK,' I said.

She gave me the egg to hold while she fitted them.

I rolled it around in my hand. It was so sparkly. I wondered what had happened to the real one. The politsiya had searched all through Victor's office, but they hadn't found it.

Maybe they never would.

Piper snapped the battery compartment shut and stood up.

'Let's go, Ollie.' She started waving the detector around. 'I have a good feeling about today. We're going to find something incredible.'

'Careful.' She'd almost whacked me!

'Sorry.'

'Why's it beeping?' I said. 'We haven't started yet.'

Piper shrugged. 'No idea.' She switched it off, and then on again.

It still beeped.

'Did yo—'

'Yes.' Piper glared at me. 'I did put the batteries in properly.'

'Maybe there's a faulty connection?' I said. 'It's quite old.'

I was just about to have a look when there was a shout from the other side of the park.

'Cooooeeee.'

'Yay!' Piper gave a little hop. 'It's your gran and Rose.'

It was. They were sprinting up the hill towards us. Grandma seemed ever-so excited about something. She waved frantically. **'Ollie? Piper?'** she screeched.

'I have news.'

Rose was racing ahead of her. What was going on? He wasn't usually that speedy. Anyone would think he hadn't seen us in months.

He charged through a clump of pampas grass and hurled himself at me.

The egg went flying.

It bounced down three of the bandstand steps and came to rest in a bed of petunias.

Oops.

I fended Rose off, and went to get it.

'Is it OK?' Piper looked anxious.

'Don't worry,' I said. I brushed off some mud. 'It's fine.'

Rose was bounding about, yapping. What was wrong with him?

'I can hear buzzing.' Piper looked around. 'Maybe it's a wasp? Rose hates them.'

I could hear buzzing too – but it wasn't a wasp.

It was the egg.

OMG. I stared at it. 'Piper,' I said. 'Look.'

'What?'

I held my hand out flat, so she could see.

The egg whirred, and then it clicked.

And then it split in two.

Something rolled out.

Blimey.

Piper blinked, and then she looked at me. 'Oh my,'

she said. 'Is that what I think it is?'

'It's SO exciting.' Grandma galloped up the path. 'The politsiya called again. You'll never guess. Viktor has given them some further intelligence.' She screeched to a halt at the bottom of the bandstand steps. 'Apparently, he hid the Moscow Star in a humbug tin, which leads me to believe, remembering what you said, Ollie, and using my exemplary powers of deduction, that the one we have, is, in fact—'

I held up an emerald the size of a pigeon's egg. 'The real thing?'

THE END

Acknowledgements

My lovely agent, **Kate Shaw**, for her constant enthusiasm and wit.

Anna Solemani, for her truly brilliant editorial skills.

Arvind Shah, designer extraordinaire.

The amazing team at **Orchard**, who have been so much fun to work with.

Nathan Reed, for the fabulous artwork.

Beryl, and the late **Mitch**, for the 1977 trip to Russia, and the inspiration. There would be no Grandma Dangerous without you.

Bath Spa Uni, and the friends I made there, for their ongoing encouragement and support.

Uffington Book Club, for the late-night literary chats.

Carineh, for making me laugh with her excellent plot ideas.

Karen Duffy, my most dangerous friend.

Claire, **Meryl**, **Jude**, **Neil**, **Lorraine**, **Rob**, **Ali**, **Vicky**, **Maia**, and **Tasha**, for only being a text away.

And finally

Isobel, **Eva**, **Hattie** and **Daisy**, for cooking their own tea when deadlines were looming.

Look out for the next book,

GRANDMA DANGEROUS

AND THE TOE OF TREACHERY!

Coming soon!

Kita Mitchell wrote and illustrated her first work, *Cindersmella*, at the age of six. It was cruelly and swiftly rejected by publishers. The sequels, *Repunsmell* and *Mouldilocks*, were equally badly received.

Disheartened, she turned her attention to making stuff, and, luckily, they did degrees in that. After getting one, she built sets for TV shows – but the feeling she should write funny books for children never went away.

Eventually, she decided to have another go. This time, things turned out a little better. Now, she can tell people she is a proper author, which is great.

Kita currently lives in Oxfordshire with four daughters and a hamster.

@kitamitchell
www.kitamitchell.com

Nathan Reed has been a professional illustrator since graduating from Falmouth College of Arts in 2000. Recent books include *How to Write Your Best Story Ever* and the *Marsh Road Mystery Series*. His latest picture book, written by Angela McAllister, is *Samson the Mighty Flea*. He was also shortlisted for the Serco Prize for Illustration in 2014.